Finding the Joy

West Australian Stories Across Time

Helene Smith

For My Family
& in memory
of those who came before

Our Mum drew water
Water more precious than gold
Woman at the well

My Dad found tweezers
Drew out the core of my pain
A man who loved tools.

Contents

Also by Helene Smith

In paperback and e-book:

Operation Clancy
Dreamstone
Leaping the Tingles
The Potter's Son

Short fiction
Flood Zone (in Xtreme Weather)

In paperback, e-book and audio format:

Children of Morwena
Aberash: A Mysterious Land Downunder.

1 Walking on Air 1955

She is seventeen with the world at her feet, catching the tram in Hay Street, avoiding the glad eye of would-be lovers. She already has a boyfriend. One with a warm cultured voice. He is tall but not too tall. Has dark wavy hair and brown eyes, with golden lights, that look right into her's. Her soldier boy is a "Nasho" and today there is a passing out parade. He sent her a telegram: *Marching down St George's Terrace at four.'*

Dizzy eyed, she is the 'chosen one', walking on air. It never once occurs to her that he might be called up to fight in some war across the sea. Oh, to be seventeen in the city with neon lights blinking, trams rattling by and the paper boys calling, 'Pee…yay ip purr. Daily news…'

There is a light rain falling, soft as snow. On days like this, her brown hair fluffs out and curls at the edges. Her skin is fresh and clear, her cheeks rosy. Her favourite patient where she nurses is from her hometown as it happens. He calls her, apple cheeks.

Happiness makes her lightheaded. Light footed. Fresh in her memory is the day when she took her boyfriend home to the farm to meet the family and their journey back to the city by train. Clickety clack…clickety clack, the warmth of his arms, swish, wish. She wanted that journey to go on forever.

Last night he said the words, 'I love you' and she's walking on air in pale blue high heeled shoes. She catches sight of herself in a shop window, pleased with her A-line dress that has been on lay-by for weeks. Ah yes, walking down Hay Street, heading for St George's Terrace. Perhaps a shilling in her purse. The man gets to pay. His wages are higher and that is the way it is. No questions asked. He'll buy her a Mint Julip on the way to the Piccadilly Theatre in Hay Street.

She has worked long hours with the telegram like a gold piece in her pocket. Smiling at patients, providing food, cups of tea and bed pans to rich, elderly patients. She wipes their bottoms and cleans up their post op vomit. Some patients are sweet, others cantankerous and demanding. She doesn't mind. Not today. She is floating on air with no need for, nor knowledge of, the hidden wings that will save her from the void. She is seventeen with the world at her feet. Her belief in fairy tales untarnished and complete.

2 Eddie William

Eddie speaks with a light in his eyes, 'I'm gettin' out o' this joint soon.'

He is in his mid-fifties, one of the younger members of the nursing home clients. He has a plan. Oh yes, he does. Sitting at the lunch table, he places his knife and fork in the centre of the plate – now empty except for a mush of greens.

'Always leave me greens.' A little boy grin lights his face. 'See yous later…I'm goin 'outside for a joint.'

With a faint swagger, he leaves the table. His joint is in fact, a cigarette, allowed under a management plan so that he doesn't run out of money before his next 'pay day'. The bulk of his pension pays for his bed and his care, leaving little for personal items.

Short in stature, Eddie is ever willing to share his story. He was a fancy ballroom dancer once, an instructor on the side. Then he worked in the building trade up north in Karratha. All day on a building site with the hot sun burning. Forty degrees or more in the shade. Separated from family, the job cost him his marriage, though he still keeps in touch with his daughter.

Afterwards, he landed a job at the local pub with lodgings thrown in. He plans to go back there. When he gets out o' this joint. 'Yep. Do a bit of work in the yard…even the bar come to think of it.' But he won't go pickin' grapes again. One season was his undoing. He and the gang travelled down south by truck to old Lorenzo's place. After work they hung around in his back shed, where the smell of fermenting grapes alone was enough to knock ya flat.

After sampling Lorenzo's hooch, they took a demijohn of the stuff to share. Every day the same. Eddie lost track of time. Days and nights bleeding into each other. The cold wind blowing in his hair and around his ears, the roadside trees and shrubbery a stream of green, the guys in the truck shouting, laughing and singing.

'I drank every day til me body said, 'Stuff ya,' he says, with a faint smile. When Eddie keeled over unconscious, his overnight girlfriend yelled for help. She soon disappeared. He remembers hands…helping hands and faces. Nursing Aides in pink uniforms feeding him. The doctor conferring with a bevy of young men and women in white coats. Days and nights flicking like shadows, until at last, he was well enough – only just – to be admitted to the nursing home.

'But soon I'll be outer here,' he says. 'Set up a little place of me own, I will.' He'll have his daughter with her partner and his grandkids come to stay. He'll fix up a nice outdoor area with a barbie. He's gonna wear one of them aprons with funny pictures on the front, and he'll cook for his family. Sausages for the kids and steak with fried onion rings for the grownups. Deep fried chips on the side and fresh bread rolls, a few tinnies, lemonade for the kids and Bob's ya uncle.

When he gets out of this joint, he's gonna get his license back first thing so he can go see his mum in the nursing home on the other side o' town. He'll bring her a big bunch of flowers. Yep, he will, and he'll go into the room with the flowers and a big grin on his face, and he'll say, 'Mum, its ya son, Eddie William.'

Eddie William is gonna take his grandkids to the zoo. They'll catch the train up to the city in the mornin' and come home that night. He'll buy 'em double headed ice creams, lollies and milk shakes. Yep, that's what he is gonna do. Soon as he gets out o' this joint.

At Easter, Eddie greets us with a grin and this time it's really gonna happen. His daughter is gonna pick him up and he's outa this joint for good. Eddie can't stop smiling and there's nothing fake. No bravado. It's real this time. The nursing home is buzzing on this day. It's Easter time and the carers are wearing Bunny Ears on their heads. There are little chocolate eggs handed out and everyone is smiling. Sunday, visitors and their kids are everywhere. Others are smiling, but none like Eddie.

Eddie's eyes are brighter than the stars. He really is gettin' out of this place and by gosh, there they are. His daughter, followed by her partner and the three grandies. Eddie's usual shuffle turns to a stride. Eddie is smiling and his daughter is smiling.

'You gettin' me outer here?' His face clouds over.

'Not that old story, Dad. But look at what we gotcha.' The daughter, small like her Dad, but rounder, holds out a huge chocolate Easter Bunny that fills her arms. For a second or two the dreadful let down reaches his sagging shoulders, but then – Eddie is smiling as best he can, greeting his grandkids and his daughter's partner.

After the excitement of Easter, winter days draws in. The bitter wind swoops around the front door of the nursing home. Family members hurry inside, away from sweeping rain and hail. Their mission, to help out at lunch time. Eddie is there with his smile and the light of hope in his eyes. Dani is a new girl in a cramped space, called a kitchen, a place in which used crockery and cutlery are washed and prepared meals handed out. Quietly spoken, she is lovely, with a special air of dignity and grace. Barely thirty, newly separated from her partner, she is a single mum of three.

Though she doesn't know it, Eddie is in love with Dani. He doesn't mind that she has three kids. He loves kids. Soon as he is out o' this joint, they'll rent a little place together and he'll make a garden of flowers for her…and a barbie for him…he'll play footy with the boy…oh he's goin' to be such a good dad to her kids, and they'll go to the city by train to watch the footy final, him and Dani and the kids. He'll buy them all double headed ice-creams.

Oh yes, he'll be out o' this joint forever, he will.

3 Running Barefooted

After all this time, I will speak of what I sensed but couldn't then articulate. You, who I knew so well, looked at me like a stranger might. I was about ten, a farm-raised kid brought to the 'big' school in town by bus when our little school closed after the war.

I was buying fruit for my lunch where you worked. You took my order as if I were a stranger. Did you recognize me? I believe you did, but it was as if you had nothing to give, as if the person that you were, had died.

Our families, yours and mine had much in common. Our mothers were teachers called back to duty for the duration of the war in little 'bush schools' and then afterwards much to our sorrow, we kids were bussed daily into one large school. Our fathers had been to war, mine in WW1 as an under-age soldier, yours in WW2. You were older than I, perhaps by six years or so, close to my brother Giles' age.

When you were teenagers you and Giles spent time together…cuddling and kissing between whispers and stifled laughter. My sisters and I would smile when you appeared from the grassy slope into the house paddock. You, barefooted and always with your little brother, Mitch on your shoulders. Sometimes your sister Roslyn came carrying red headed Johnny. Dear little post war babes and their big sisters.

One day Roslyn sang when we other children were *quiet enough to hear a pin drop* as our teacher-mother would say. The pure sweet sound captured my soul. I had never heard it before, but the song and her voice stayed with me.

> *Beautiful dreamer…queen of my song…beauti-*
> *ful dreamer awake unto me…*

You and Roslyn came to us in your bare feet.

When I saw you in the greengrocer, you were newly married. You hardly greeted me at all and I felt a stab of disappointment. It was as if the Rachel I knew had been spirited away. Her face, once so full of light and laughter, now bitter and sad. There were rumours about your jealous man, 'pulling you into line'. He was a little below average in height, but with a good physique and a sullen kind of beauty.

On that day in the veggie shop I took the fruit from you and handed over the money. Our exchange (or lack of it) gave me a sick feeling in my soul. I couldn't explain what I felt, even to myself. A kind of disappointment in friendship and human relationships generally. What came to me as I trudged back to school was quite a different image of you.

It was on Show Day when everyone in town celebrated with stalls and parades, horse races, people cheering, and a merry-go-round with an exotic male keeper with black, shoulder length hair and eyes, dark and mysterious as a deep water well. I have a vague recollection of my own white muslin dress, starched and ironed for the occasion. My hair in ringlets after being set in 'rags' the night before. On that day, I was some distance away, but like Roslyn's song, the sight of you, would stay with me always.

You in a calf length dress in pale mauve *crepe de chine*. It was 'the new look' that set you among the stars. Your shoulder length, honey blonde hair topped with a big picture hat and matching wedgy shoes. To me, you looked like a film star. As we ate sandwiches under the shade of the pine trees, I heard a jealous remark about you by one of the older girls and I bristled. *Catty witch,* I knew more about you than she did.

I think of you today, wondering about your life. I know you had children and something tells me you would have been a wonderful mother. As for your husband…perhaps you learned to pacify the hurt child within the beast. You might forgive the person, but never the act which has a way of lingering in the mind. Or, for your children's sake and your inner peace, I hope you found a way to nurture the joyful self that I and my siblings knew when you and your sister tripped into our lives with your bare feet swishing through the long green grass.

4 The Gold Fob Watch

Reginald Jacob Robinson. With the tip of his forefinger, Jake
traces his father's name. The watch has touched his dad.
Now he has touched the watch – for the very first time.
A fob watch they said. Forty carat gold, they said. Expen-
sive, but that isn't the point. Jake was born after his daddy
died.

Trembling, he slips the watch into the cocoon of its
black velvet box, closes the lid and stuffs it into the lined
pocket of his school trousers. A feathery weight brushing
lightly against his thigh. His daddy in a box. A sliver of
excitement and fear runs through his nine-year old body.
Taller than the other kids in his class, his limbs loose and
gangly, a reason for Jake to make himself small.

'For heaven's sake straighten up, lad,' says Mr Randle.
The kids tease Jake about looking like a dumb clodhop-
per and they'll tease him again at the end of the day when
he stays behind to help Mum clean the school. It is Jake's
job to open all the windows and then close them afterwards. The kids mock him, as he carries the slop bucket
or wipes away their sticky finger marks from the walls.
Between jobs he'll be alone while his mum is off somewhere with a heavy broom sweeping classroom
floorboards. That's when he feels it – the weirdness of a

school, when after the clatter of a busy day, it turns into something else.

Jake knows the pervasive smell of chalk dust in his nostrils and those long corridors full of shadows and strange echoes. They will swoop and sigh like ghosts. Are there ghosts in the school at the end of the day? This was his Daddy's school too – is he here?

But it is morning now, Jake thinks, and the sun is shining. People are going to work. The streets are busy. No ghost would want to be here. But you never know, a voice tells him and so he touches the velvet box in his pocket. *It's only for a lend…just for one day.*

After school he might show Lionel the watch and then go straight to Granma's house. While she's taking the washing off the line, he'll sneak into her bedroom and put daddy back where he belongs. Jake joins the long straggly line into the classroom and remembers the homework he hasn't done. If he gets the cuts for it, he won't cry. He'll be brave because he has daddy.

His daddy in a box.

As it happens, Mr Randle doesn't ask about homework. *Thank you for that, Daddy.* It feels weird but nice talking to daddy in his head.

Unlike Jake, his sisters Emma and Freya and older brother, Alec know what it was like to have a dad. To talk to him for real. They are at high school and will grumble about Parents' Day. With dad gone and mum who thinks Parents' Day is a lot of nonsense, they are told to sit on the seat outside while the other kids show off their work to their parents. Emma says they feel like silly drongos sitting there all afternoon.

Aunty Olive reckons their mum is a *looker,* whatever that means. Says she could meet somebody…that she's far too tight lipped and proud to do anything but work, weekends and all. No widow's pension for Jake's mum. No welfare man looking into her cupboards to see that she's not starving her kids. Or looking under her bed to see if a pair of man's shoes lurk there. Weird, that one. Why would she have a pair of a man's shoes under her bed?

The early morning buzz of the classroom turns to silence. There are sums on the board this morning. Too easy. Jake grins. He is fast with numbers. Knows the price of things in pounds, shillings and pence. Can add up and take away, divide and multiply.

In Class Five, he's gonna learn fractions. Sometimes for fun he copies Freya whose studying for her Junior Certificate and will chant, 'The square on the hypotenuse is equal to the squares on the other two sides.' Hypotenuse sounds a bit like the animal he's only seen in the pages of Britannica. It makes him giggle to think of it. A big red square sitting on top of a hippopotamus with its huge jaw wide open and two squares, smaller by half, hanging down on either side.

At recess Lionel grabs his arm. 'Hey, Jake do you wanna play footy with the big kids?' Lionel is his friend. Small but fast on the footy field and full of tricks. Jake nearly gives way, but feels that small feathery weight against his thigh.

'Nar, don't wanna, today,' he drawls. Every time the pair go on to the footy field there's a rough tangle of arms and legs. He'll cop a kick in the shins or his shirt collar might be torn. He can't risk dropping the gold watch. Worse still, having the big kids gawking at it.

No. He'll show it to Lionel this arvo and have a quick gink himself before heading for Grandma's house to put it back where he found it. Then he'll gaze at the photo of his daddy in the hallway. It's the first thing anyone sees when they come. Aunty Olive will always whisper in his ear, 'You're the spitting image of him at the same age, Jake.' So, he might grow to be like that, a handsome man with "soulful" dark eyes – no longer as he is now – all bones, gawky and clumsy. Like the ugly duckling in the story before he turns into a swan.

Later Jake will remember it like a terrible dream…the two police cars in the driveway of Granma's house. His mother, running in from their house next door. Tight lipped, her eyes read him. As if she can see right into his skull. As if she might crush his wild pumping heart. Icy fingers of fear run down his spine.

There's been a robbery…the precious gold watch has been taken. How does she know its him? He swallows down a great lump in his throat. How? Her hand is a vice. Tight round his wrist, pre-empting his attempt to draw the watch from his pocket. She prizes it from his frozen fingers, slapping it onto the table.

'It was just for a lend,' he wails.

'You shamed me.' Her words are ice.

Jake's mum isn't his mum now, but a demon, a

banshee, dragging him home, pulling him into the boys' room on the end of the veranda. She grabs Alec's scouts' belt with its hard buckle, laid so innocently beside a washed and ironed scout uniform. Without pity, she lays into her son. Lays into him with the weight of her own anger and grief.

Nine years' worth of pay-back to an absent husband, foolish enough to die before his time. Not a death covered in the glory of a Gallipoli, but a stupid car crash that should never have happened. It is pay-back to the townspeople waiting for her to trip up. For the men at the hotel when she serves them – their sly pinches and comments. And to Jake who reminds her every day of all she has lost, a son who has shamed her. And to the goddamn fucking everyday struggle of life itself.

Jake will remember until he is an old man – the sting of the scout belt. The buckle at one end that cuts his calves and clips his cheek. He manages to pull away from her briefly, jumping from his own bed onto Luke's and back again. His quick evasion and surprising strength infuriate her.

For a brief moment, Jake sees Freya's alarmed face at the window, vaguely aware that she has been banging on the locked door.

'Enough…enough,' she screams at their mother and within seconds his darling sister is through the window wrenching the belt from their mother's hand.

They never speak of it but it is Freya who cleans him up. Freya who comforts him. Time passes, one day after another. Weeks run into months and then years. Other events will fade from Jake's mind, but that one stays.

An uncle fits Jake up with a bike and after school he cycles to the fishing harbour. Earns a few shillings helping old Mac who gives him a snapper head to take home for tea. He shoves it in a sugar bag that does for a swag and carries it home slung across his back. Sometimes, it's a whole snapper. Today when he arrives home, Freya tells him, 'You pong of fish guts.'

'Do not,' he says, grinning. But he'll take a shower. He likes to be clean. Likes to be neat. Jake sometimes helps out at the drapery store. The customers love him. That handsome Robinson kid…who would have thought it? And a good head for business too.

Without speaking, Mum puts the fish head into a pot of water. Chops up an onion and herbs from the garden. As it simmers on the Metta's stove top, light from the firebox plays on pretty rose printed curtains, chosen and hung by Jake. He has an eye for colour and style.

Now that Luke has moved away to share a farm with an uncle, Jake takes his place at the head of the table. Soon he'll be earning a full wage. Freya and Emma are working girls now. Freya in the office at the Trading company, Emma in the chemist. Both have boyfriends – sons of wheat and sheep farmers.

Jake thinks he'll give the Junior Certificate exam a miss and leave school to work in the drapery. On the weekend there is sport. Mum never comes to watch him play but takes good care of his clothes. His whites always snowy and his trophies shine bright in the new china cabinet the girls bought her. His photograph is on the wall now – grinning, holding up the trophy for fairest and best.

When there is a fund-raising event in the township Jake knows what must be done. He is needed and in demand. Something else is happening in his life as well. The family doesn't know yet, but he's fallen in love. Her name is Judy. Sweet faced Judy with her big blue eyes and neat shining hair. Generous hearted. When Jake is an old man Judy will mourn when she and their three loving children fade from his memory – so quickly, without warning. So too, their home with its shining surfaces, the copper etchings, the knick-knacks Jake himself has chosen, the flower garden he attended so lovingly. All will fade from his mind.

It is his mother and that first home he sees in his mind's eye.

'I need to go home,' he will say, blindly pushing his walker. 'Where is Mum, is she okay?'

5 A Tiny Light

It was mid-winter, 1950 when the Sweeny family heard the news. Elsie, wife of Brad Morris, has given birth to a baby boy at the Manji hospital.

'Born in the early hours,' Jan Sweeny tells her family. The young couple have taken over the old Group Settlement place down the road. Jan loves the idea of the district coming to life again. Thank God the war years are over. Brad is a returned serviceman. Now a farmer and a dad. It makes Jan smile.

The weatherboard farmhouse rattles in the wind and a smattering of rain beats down on the iron roof as she dishes up beef stew and the requisite 'three veggies' for her brood – three boys and three girls. Breast fed as babies, each and every one. Now sturdy youngsters round the family table. Hers came so easily – a bit too easily she thinks, ruefully. She loves and is proud of each one, delighting in their individual personalities.

If only Stan might feel the same sense of purpose in raising their family as she does. In time his condition will be labelled, the "Black dog" or some fancy Latin name that means depression, but for Stan and his bewildered family in the 1950's it has no name. He sits for hours with hunched shoulders, his handsome ruddy face withdrawn.

Reluctantly he moves to the table but he has no appetite. Jan's own stomach clenches with worry as she puts the knife and fork in his hands. But when she picks up her own, a loud knock on the back door has her on her feet.

'It's only me, Mrs Sweeny,' a voice calls above the lashing wind.

'Brad! Do come in and have a bite to eat…I heard the good news. You have a son…congratulations!' Jan is already devising a quick plan to halve her own untouched meal. With left over mashed potato and gravy, it will be something to offer their unexpected guest. She turns to face him with a smile of welcome which quickly falls away. 'Oh, dear Brad, what is it?'

'Mrs Sweeny…Jan…it's the baby…We're going to lose him.' In a broken voice Brad goes on, 'Doctor Bill thinks he's…a…a blue baby…and it's too late to do anything.' He holds back tears. "I need to be with my wife.' The message was sent via a neighbour who dropped it into Brad's mailbox without realising the gravity of its content.

His words come haltingly, 'I wonder…I wonder if Stan would mind taking me into the hospital on his motorbike?' While the question hangs in the air, Jan is acutely aware of her children. Their eyes are fixed on her face. In silence they wait. She turns to Stan, his face self-absorbed, vaguely hostile. Beyond that, she sees the lonely depth of his sad isolation. Like something deep and dark as ink. How do you break through such a stark barrier?

'Of course, Stan will take you, Brad,' Jan says.

She senses the children looking on, transfixed, as she grabs Stan's coat from a hook on the wall. As she pulls at his arms until he stands. As she guides his arms through the sleeves of the overcoat, fastens it with the belt and pulls it tightly. As she propels him – with Brad following, towards the door.

Jan nods to their older boy, Tommy, and as if a spell has been broken, the children finish their meals and hurry to clean up, for once without argument. Tommy lights the hurricane lamp, his boy-man hands shaking a little as he shelters the flaring match head and then holds it to the wick. With lamp in hand, Jan stands while Stan kick starts the motorcycle. It ticks over smoothly like always. Stan has a way with engines.

When they drive away, Jan concentrates on one thing alone…that tiny light from the motorcycle slicing through the blustery night. She wishes fervently for Brad to reach the hospital before his little son breathes his last breath. She mourns that baby as the light flickers between long shadows cast by the overarching gum trees along the gravel road.

'Come back safely,' Jan whispers to her troubled man. He will be frozen when he returns, good reason to keep the kitchen stove burning. She will have hot cocoa ready and toast spread liberally with lashings of butter.

6 The Door

Mum is here in Seaside Town and so am I. Today I'm going to find her, Linda tells her ten-year-old self. World War II has ended. Victory day is done and Linda knows her mum is no longer needed to help with the war effort.

All she has is a half-remembered glimpse of a house from when she was quite small. A house with a door that towered above her. Tall and solemn. But there was something special about that door that made her remember it. What was it?

Gazing into the mirror in Mrs Allen's bathroom, Linda splashes another handful of water on to her long brown hair and brushes it thoroughly. With careful precision, she pulls it behind and secures it with an elastic band. Quite a tricky process. But there it is. Plain and neat. Fringed with thick black lashes, she sees the mirror image of her deep blue eyes. Eyes so intense, people rarely notice anything else about her – not the neat floral dress with pale green buttons or the sensible boy sandals that Grandpa insists upon.

Today you must find Mum's house, Linda, she tells herself sternly. In the kitchen Mrs Allen is snappish, but not unkind…just too busy with hard work to bother with a child. Right now, she skims off the clotted cream from a big pot of cold scalded milk.

Her florid face turns to Linda. 'Now you've done your chores, you can go outside and play, but do go quietly.' Linda knows Mr Allen and the two grown-up sons need a quiet sleep in the daytime because they're fisherman and work most nights.

'Don't go off by yourself,' Mrs Allen tells her. 'Stay close with your friends.'

When in Seaside Town, Linda is allowed to play with the O'Hara or the Manolio kids who live nearby. At present she is boarding with Mrs Allen, a distant cousin of Grandpa's. He arranged it to give poor Grandma a rest. Grandpa arranges everything, every time.

But not this time. Linda swallows down a flutter of anticipation and fear. She will call in to see the Manolios and O'Haras. Of course she will, but today she is going to find her mum's house. If not today then the day after. She counts down from seven. Five days left. Five whole days when Grandpa doesn't arrange anything. Five whole days to find her mum's house.

Linda closes Mrs Allen's door softly and then shuts the gate with a satisfying clunk. Before her and behind, sleepy old Seaside Town sprawls outwards to the Indian Ocean, with houses on both sides of a thinly bituminised road. On the vacant block near their home, the Manolio tribe and friends use bits of tin or card for a free fast ride down a steep earth slope. Only George bothers to say hello.

'Want to have a shot?' he asks.

She shakes her head.

Further along the street, in between teasing and loud laughter, the O'Hara girls sit on the grass in front of their house making daisy chains or plucking out the petals chanting and arguing. *He loves me, he loves me not...ah you love him too...he's your boyfriend...no he's not...yes, he is...*

'Want to come swimming with us?' Alma asks.

'I'm going to the shops for Mrs Allen,' says Linda.

With her money purse in a handstitched cotton bag looped over her shoulder, Linda walks into the day alone. Her day – a hazy blur of dusty white and pale blue, solidifying into limestone walls, a hint of sea, the sound of gulls soaring. On dry grass verges, magpies scrounge for seeds and insects. Houses cheek to cheek. Which one is Mum's? Which one? What was so special about that door? Linda stops now and then to keep track of her bearings. She has sketched out a map with an indelible pencil on a sheet of plain white wrapping paper begged from the butcher.

By one o'clock, Linda's face is hot and sweaty. Her hair, having escaped the elastic band, flops over her face annoyingly. Thankfully she makes her way to a public change room near the beach for a wee and to take a long drink from the tap with her cupped hand.

Nearby is a bakery with its delicious fresh bread smell. With the money earned from selling lemonade bottles at home, she agonises between custard tarts and sausage rolls. One of each, she decides and adds a packet of Irish Moss for the long haul. More hours searching. Tomorrow she vows to wear the sunhat Grandma made for her. Even if it does make her look like a dope, it keeps the blazing sun from her face.

More footwork until late afternoon when friendly shadows stroke Linda's sun burned skin and in a magical moment she glimpses the pale sea, now turned to gold. Oh, but she is tired. Wearily, Linda trudges home to Mrs Allen. She forgets to ask if she might listen to the Argonauts Club on the wireless, but will help bring in clothes from the washing line and set the table for tea. Fork on the left, knife on the right and dessert spoon across the top. Neat.

For tea, there is corned beef covered with white sauce, fresh garden peas and a good dollop of mashed spuds. It is followed by jam tart and custard, a favourite, but Linda struggles to stay awake long enough to eat it. After helping with dishes, a quick face, hands and feet wash and she crawls into bed in a half stupor, only to dream and dream.

In this way, the days pass. Every day impatient to be free from chores. Free from other kids and making excuses with small white lies. Free to hunt for that one house, that one door and nights dreaming about doors. Unpainted doors, shiny doors, doors with knockers and fancy letter slots. Doors with stained glass windows, but not the right one.

So often an image comes into her head, a wispy thread to tease her. A vague swirl of colour: birds and leaves…vibrant red…lapis blue…leafy green…Is that it? Is that Mum's door?

Everyday Linda's eyes, after ten years of seeing, intensely blue, fringed with black lashes, searching. Searching for a house, a door. Searching for her mum…the house…the door. It isn't until the very last day that Linda leaps out of bed before Mrs Allen is awake, even before Mr Allen and the boys arrive home from their night's work. Today is the day, of this she is sure.

Before leaving the house, Linda scrounges for a bowl of Wheaties and because her pocket money is running low, makes herself a plum jam sandwich for lunch, careful to cut the bread straight and to clean up after herself, hoping Mrs Allen won't be cross with her.

Quietly, she opens the back door and steps into the garden to pick the two nearly ripe nectarines she spotted a few days earlier. The dunny truck has left the gate to the back laneway open. For that reason, it is almost by chance that Linda exits Mrs Allen's house from the back. It leads to shady street trees and a mix of semi-detached and stand-alone houses. And something more. A strong feeling. *Like I've been here before.* This is it.

This is the street. A surge of excitement courses through her and then a great calmness and certainty. Linda pictures her mum's house. Free standing and on this street. She skips past several semi-detached places. One, two more houses and she stands still, hardly daring to breathe.

There it is. Mum's house with a door etched indelibly in her memory. A door that haunted her dreams. A tall dark door, a frowning solemn door until you look up. The stained-glass inset is alight with bright green leaves held together by a curved central stem and on either side, small birds — ruby red on one, lapis blue on the other.

In an agony of shyness, Linda can't bring herself to knock, but she will wait. She will wait until the end of time if she must, sitting on the grass in the shade of a street tree on the verge. Lynda worries that her mum won't even know she has been. Worries that her mum is inside the house. The dark house. Alone. Sad. Is she crying — that slow kind of grown-up sobbing that goes on and on? Linda pushes away a memory, threadlike and slippery as a worm.

Time drags. A stray tabby cat comes to lean against her, purring contentedly when she scratches it behind the ears. 'I'm going to stay until I can be sure Mum is okay,' she tells him. 'I'll stay for today and tomorrow and the day after until I know.'

A grey-haired lady with a shopping bag in each hand comes by. 'Are you okay, love?' she asks.

'Just waiting for a friend,' Linda bites her lip. When the cat trots away, she feeds crumbs from her stale sandwich to a hungry magpie. The nectarines she keeps for herself. Crunchy and thirst quenching. Time seems to stand still, the air frowzily thin and hazy white. Linda falls into a half dream until once again gentle shadows of late afternoon touch her. Fully awake, her intense blue eyes narrow as she looks at the door. Just as Linda knows it will happen, there are footsteps. Tap, tap, tap on the wooden floor. Does she see someone else in the shadows? Hear a man's voice calling her mother's name? In time she will ask herself these questions but for now everything but her mum is eclipsed.

She stands on the porch with eyes just like her own.

But her mum is a breath-of-fresh-air. Beautiful. Like a movie star. Her hair a shining blonde bob, set off by glittering drop earrings, a slender neck and fine head. Her green silk dress, shimmers like a waterfall, from a low-cut neck, all the way down to dainty gold sandals. No boy sandals for her mum. She wears bright red lipstick but she is not smiling. Her voice is low and tense, almost a whisper. Both scary and scared.

'Linda, you must not come here. Please. Go back. Go back to Mrs Allen's house and…don't come again…please.'

Linda runs from the woman who is her mother with eyes like her own. Runs from the house and the door. Linda runs until, simply to go on breathing, she needs to stop. To lean forward, taking in great gulps of air. It is only when her breath evens out, when her heart stops thumping, that she sits. She sits for a long time on a park bench.

There's just me now, she thinks. *Me and the tree and the sky and the grass.* And then, like a new day, it comes. Pin pricks of fresh energy in her fingertips all the way to her toes. Gosh she is hungry and Mrs Allen is having roast lamb for tea. She will need Linda to pick the juicy tips of mint plants in the garden to make sauce.

Tonight is her last night with Mrs Allen, that's why they are having a roast (and it's not even Sunday). Tomorrow she'll go back on the train to Grandma.

'I wanted to see my mum, and I did,' she tells the cooling air. Linda is not sorry. She will never be sorry that she found her Mum's house. *All by myself too, and I was right about that door!* She takes a deep breath and stands, ready to go back to Mrs Allen's now. Linda imagines boasting a little to her friend at school. About her beautiful mum who looks like a movie star. *Maybe one day when Grandpa is busy doing farm work, I'll tell Granma or someone…about finding my Mum's house…maybe…*

7 Flowers

Hilda's thin lips draw in to a tight knot. 'Take them out. I told you not to bring flowers. They give me hay fever and that will lead to bronchitis. Is that what you want?'

'But Ma,' Gareth says. 'Remember? Last year on Mother's Day we were in trouble for not bringing you flowers.' Surreptitiously, he caresses my lower back as if to remind me of our night of lovemaking.

Hilda sniffs, 'You came with Flora Tilburg last year. I'm sure you did.'

Gareth shakes his head. 'I'm with Evie now, Mum. We're married remember?'

She throws me a look. Half amused. Sure, of her ground, yet watchful. As if to observe and make a note of my discomfort. 'You came with Flora Tilburg, for sure.' Indifferent to the topic of flowers now and gushing a little, Hilda offers Gareth the local newspaper and a nice cup of tea. Carefully made with real leaf tea…drawn for a good little while. Just the way he likes it.

'There's your chair close to the fire, Gareth,' she goes on, 'and a cushion for that back of yours.'

I am left feeling foolish, still clutching the flowers with one hand. The other is spread across my rising belly. For the first time in my pregnancy, I feel clumsy and heavy. It is all so new to me. I'm full of questions and fears. I

can't find the words to explain. At times I stammer inef-
fectively or keep silent. My bladder feels like it's going to
burst and I head for the toilet, wondering if last night's
mammoth love making was really such a smart thing to
do.

*Gareth still desires me and he loves me — of course he does —
loves me.* I say the word to myself like a mantra.
Love…love will overcome everything…won't it? To love
or learn to make and love a whole new family…that is
the question. Even love Hilda? But Hilda doesn't even
like me. I push the thought away. Unlike me, Gareth is
totally at ease in his mother's household. He is older than
I am. Comfortable in his own skin. Absorbed now in
reading the paper, exchanging a few words with his mum.
She has taken the second easy chair beside him and is
working on her crossword. If I join them, I will need to
choose a heavy dining chair on the other side of the table.
It won't occur to Gareth to find me one. He is used to
being waited on in this house.

Tears sting my eyes. 'Stupid,' I scold myself and leave
the room with the offending flowers. A few steps and I
am through the enclosed back veranda. The flywire door
twangs behind me and I breath fresh air redolent with the
scent of my flowers. Stocks. An ugly name for such a
sweet- smelling beauty. Way back in the summertime, I
worked in the hot sun, digging out the garden bed from
the hard clay soil at the front of our rented house, filling
it with well-rotted manure from the chook yard. Barrow
load after barrow load. Patiently waiting for the weather
to break and the soil, well-cured and ready, before

planting the tiny slips I raised from seed.

'I will go on planting flowers,' I tell myself. A glittering burst of winter sunshine lights the day. Beyond Hilda's back yard the rural township nestles serenely in and around the hills. With bushland close by, there are birds — magpies carolling, the sweet whisperings of wrens and a warbler is singing its little heart out. A flock of twenty-eight parrots fly in to squabble and scrounge among the fruit trees next door.

An orange tree hanging over the fence offers a great swathe of fruit. Bright orange baubles against a nest of greenery. But suddenly I am staring at a person and I cannot look away. A woman, older than I am by ten years or so. Like a physical blow, her grief-stricken face cuts right into me.

'Mrs Morgan?' I whisper.

'Oh please. Please call me Loraine.' We stare at each other. I, not yet twenty. Young. Untried. What did I have to offer but a kind of blind faith in life itself? I don't know anything, and I'm feeling more ignorant and inadequate by the day. Shouldn't I make polite conversation and then excuse myself? I search her face without speaking, taking in the unspoken message in her eyes and in the soft contours of her face. Not beautiful but full of feeling. It cries out to me. *Please see me. Hear me. Make me real. Don't pass me by.* Like somebody rehearsing a speech. Or waking from a dream to find herself in the real world, before asking, 'Would you, like to help yourself to oranges?'

'Yes,' I say, but would you…like some flowers?' I too, sound stiff and unnatural. As I pass the bouquet into her hands, I am surprised at the delicacy and softness of her fingers.

'Stocks. How wonderful.' She holds the blooms close and we stand there with the jagged ends of the broken fence between us. The chattering parrots fly away and for a moment there is silence.

The woman lifts her face and speaks. 'It's like these flowers came down from heaven, just now.'

I wait without speaking and she goes on.

'I've been ill…far too ill to take care of my boy and my home. I've lost custody of him. I've lost everything.' Her gaze shifts from my face to the flowers. 'I'm taking a few personal things…then I'm leaving…She makes a gesture with her shoulders. 'My husband, Gerrard…he has found somebody else.'

I swallow a great lump in my throat as I watch her dropping her head once again to the waiting blooms, taking in the sweetness of their scent.

8 Steak and Kidney Pie

All his rage is directed at Leah who floats on the day, serenely smiling at their younger boy. Rob's temper rises, his hold onto the small world he knows, slippery. Puts a six-pack of beer in the fridge, slams it shut. Hard. Leah hears, though she remains determinedly civil.

'Oh great, you were able to get the kidney and the lard for his pie. Did you hear that, Johnny? I'll clear the table and you can start cooking right away.'

Steak and kidney pie. Warm and meaty. An English dish for a cold winter day. Johnny wants to make a pie like the one in the story he is reading. He doesn't care that this town lies well past the 26th parallel. It is never cold, even in the wet with the river running hard. But he wants to make that pie and Dad has bought the ingredients.

Dad always buys the stores on a Saturday. Everyone helps bring them in. Mum too, and then she packs them away. Gee, this is pretty good. Mum has tidied up already and turned the oven on. They read the recipe together before he lines up the ingredients like she told him. He washes his hands thoroughly before rubbing butter and some lard into the flour. The Landrover starts up again and backs out of the driveway. Dad has stalked around for a bit and then gone out. He's been pretty grumpy about finding kidneys and lard (of all bloody things) on the shopping list.

Rob rounds the corner and parks the car near the pub. He has never really connected with the locals here. In the past it was what he did. He'd stay all afternoon and most evenings. If he was pissed off at home or at work, it was somewhere to go. Darts, pool. He is good at games. He has a fast tongue and likes to cross verbal swords with his peers. Women. Always a few around though never a priority for him. Not that he's ever crossed the line but he enjoys the banter especially with an attractive woman. He is still something of a looker himself. Still trim and on a Friday after work there had been work colleagues to relax with, mostly women. One or two had fallen for him — their mentor and boss. Made no secret of it. But in this damn town, there is no one. Spending hours in the pub no longer works for him.

Most nights now it is drinking cans of beer at home with no 'sparring partners' just the wife, watching the ABC on TV with two fidgety pre-teen boys who can't keep bloody still or quiet for more than five minutes. He pushes back memories of the year just past in another more congenial township. His aged mother's death. He hasn't shed a tear, though she has always been part of his life. He had been her whole life. It was the sight of her teaspoons in the drawer that made him want to…what? Cry?

He shut that gate pretty smartly, didn't he? Got really angry. Gave Leah a verbal lashing. In a weird way, it helped that friends were present to hear him point out her faults. A kind of buffer. Easier than face to face. They'd see what he had to put up with. How dare she put his mother's teaspoons with the others? How dare she?

Rob's thoughts drift to another ending in that same year. Another loss. He'd fallen in love. A workplace colleague. Easy to talk to. She felt the same way about him, but they never crossed the line and he only kissed her the once. Everyone was leaving and singing that soppy song about leavings. Bloody song. It was just the one passionate kiss and the look they exchanged. In front of his wife. That makes it alright, doesn't it? In a weird kind of way. Nothing hidden. Maybe he'd kissed his wife and looked at her like that once. He supposes so. Another thought to brush away.

Johnny hears the Landrover door slam. It is Dad back home. He hasn't stayed at the pub for long. He opens the six pack and takes one out. Spreads the paper across the table and gulps beer straight from the can. You can tell he is furious with mum. While they wait for the pie to turn a nice crispy brown, Johnny thinks about the story again. An adventure with heroes and villains. Clear cut. He likes a story that cuts to the chase.

Not like everyday life with no clean-cut lines. Everyday life is all fuzzy at the edges. Mum is proud of him for making the pie. But Dad is mad at Mum for being so pleased about it. This, after he criticised her for not running a tight ship. No discipline. There are angry words with Dad going on about Mum, and Mum saying she is trying her best, trying to encourage her kids.

Dad doesn't say if he enjoyed the pie. He doesn't eat much at all. Afterwards, he goes to bed for a lie-down and they are told to be quiet and not bounce the ball outside the bedroom window. Mum does something quite unusual that day. She goes for a walk by herself and for a very long time.

Dad has a lot of beer to sleep off. Quietly, brother Luke puts the empty cans on the roof, in strict order for easy counting. It is like he has a plan or is storing up evidence. After everything has kind of settled back and Dad calms down, Mum tells them about her adventure.

In time Johnny gets the picture. Mum wading through the water with her bucket, fishing knife and a bit of bate on a line. Mum, with the sky a pale dome above her and the dark iridescent blue of the waters, the river and tide doing their dance, as she will say. There are islands of greenery in the wide riverbed with wild passionfruit vines and bush tomatoes in various stages of ripeness creeping over the trees and shrubs.

Leah hears herself make light of her day, pushing down her uneasiness. It is quite usual for her to explore new surroundings when Rob has a new posting, especially before she is able to find part-time work for herself. Usually with one or both boys. But this time she is alone. Rob wants her to 'butt out' and leave the boys to him.

When the river water dwindles near the cut, she walks bare footed over the crunchy red sand. Being Saturday, the sporting fields and the pubs are packed. There are not many people fishing. Leah can't keep her eyes off those deep tidal pools.

'You'll find a big blue manna in every one,' a voice says. A man of about forty with sandy hair, and an open weathered face. Light blue eyes and work roughened hands. He grins and makes a thumbs up sign when she lands not only a big crab but a large flathead, using the knife to give it a quick death.

'So, where on earth did you come from?' he asks, smiling, and she realises he is puzzled by her sudden appearance. 'You've walked a bloody long way, and the tide is coming in again…do you…need a lift home?' He looks down at her bare feet.

What did they talk about? She thinks he might have remarked that he was among the crowd that recently watched the river come down after rain up-country. He might have expressed his wonder at nimble-fingered Aboriginal boys. How each one would snatch up a fish from the wiggling throng that appeared magically where no river had been a day before. With quick fingers the captured fish was hooked to a cord round his waist. Leah had been there with Rob and the boys that day, mesmerised by the swirling waters. The sound of it tick, tick, ticking. Its power. She wonders if the man has a family. He works up-country on a sheep station, he tells her.

The feeling of uneasiness about getting into the man's jeep is not about the stranger. It is her fear of Rob's reaction to it. One more reason for rejection and angst? When she asks to be dropped off near the shop, a street away from home, she is even more uneasy. What if Rob happens to see her or a neighbour mentions it to him?

He will think she is hiding something. Best to be up front and open about her day. To live from day to day as best she can.

When Johnny hears Mum come home, he and Luke hug her. Smiling in a forced way she tells them about her adventure. She cooks the crab but nobody wants to eat it, especially Dad, who is the only one who really likes crab meat. Mum makes cold meat and salad for tea and they all sit down to eat in a strained kind of silence. It has been a crap day really, Johnny thinks. He'll start his new library book and read in bed. As for his grand idea – *bugger steak and kidney pie*. If it makes everyone so miserable and narky, he won't make it again.

9 The Smile

Jack's face reflects back to him. Receding hairline, sallow, sun damaged skin. Lines of suffering etched into cheeks and forehead. The bleak sadness of his eyes. When they tear up, he washes away the evidence, drying his face and hands with the nursing home's unbleached paper towelling. He's conscious of the coarse stubble on his chin. In his hurry to feed her at lunch time, he forgot to shave. But what the hell…

In the room proper, Grace sleeps. He's thankful the carers have taken steps to stop her slipping into that awkward position where her whole-body collapses and she is in pain. Gently, Jack smooths strands of silver white hair away from her face.

'My darling.'

When she wakens he will brush it with a super soft brush from the set. His first gift to her, the prettiest object he could find in the general store near his farm. It was a meeting place, close neighbour to the pub where you might sit and wait for the Albany doctor to come in – that amazing rush of cool air after its long journey from the sea. It will stir the salmon gums, already turned to gold by the setting sun. Grace. His Grace. That's where they met. Jack, shy farmer, in awe of her fine boned features. The smoothness of her face and the welcoming brilliance of her smile. How hard he works for it now. The smile that opened a door for him — a widower, in deep mourning when he met her. And she, divorcee with a generous hearted grown-up daughter.

Together the life-loving pair lifted him from grief-stricken days when he thought love and intimacy had gone from his life forever. She led. She showed him. How to truly love and be loved. Now they are a family.

Jack knows, by those fleeting shifts in a person's facial expression, that the medicos have given up on her. In his mind's eye, the grave faces of specialists parade before him and even his kindly GP advised, 'Find your nearest nursing home for the care she will need.'

Jack shifted locations to be near her, but he has not given up on her and by God, he's gonna find somebody to help her. The ex-farmer will give anyone who will listen, a blow-by-blow account of his struggle. He will speak of some test he thinks Grace might have or some report on Google that suggests hopeful research and a possible cure. At the same time, he is acutely sensitive to disbelief, pity, the blank stare of incomprehension or boredom and will turn away mid-sentence.

Grace stirs and he holds her hand, willing the warmth of his own blood and the eagerness of his heart to flow into hers. Then it comes, just for him, this once, without effort. The twinkling bluest of blue eyes where the brilliance of her smile begins.

10 Plumage

It is all because of a bird, Bridie tells herself. *A bird? Really?* Her mind opens to the moment, just an hour ago, in the hair salon across the way. Only half listening to the hairdresser's story, but pleased the girl recently walked out on a cheating skunk of a man called Jarrad. Found a place of her own and reconnected with her parents. What courage. She will own her own hair salon one day.

'Good on you Marisa…well done…' Blissfully removed from her own concerns, Bridie closes her eyes while turning on the massage option of the leather chair beneath her. She is having the hair makeover thanks to her sister's sage advice.

'You're growing old and don't like it. We're all growing old. It's a condition for living don't you know? Go have a trendy haircut…and meet the old friends you've been neglecting.'

'I guess you're right, and good for the economy after Covid.' Bridie manages a final 'okay' with optimism blooming in her heart after a rare fit of the miseries.

She expects that some of her old friends will already be gathering at the café across the way. With eyes closed, she senses that buzz of anticipation from the mixed-up sounds of a busy shopping centre. Her friends are a conservative lot for sure. Tastefully dressed seniors in muted shades. Favour natural fabrics over synthetics and buy comfortable leather shoes. For one or two there might be an overseas holiday planned if not a hip replacement.

As if in recovery after minor surgery herself, Bridie rises from her torpor within the beauty saloon's chair.

'There you go,' Marisa beams at her and then frowns. 'Oh! Oh no, I'm so sorry, I was operating on automatic – thinking of Jarrad. You won't like it…unless…no, course you won't like it.' Her lips tremble. A flush creeps across her face. Her dark eyes threaten tears. 'Please…please don't say anything to my boss…'

In heavy silence they stare at Bridie's image until Marisa finds her voice. 'Do you think I was too hard on my Jarrad?'

My Jarrad indeed. 'A rotten cheater gets what he deserves,' Bridie says while considering the implications of the spectre before her. 'Marisa…I'm a grandmother, a great grandmother. How can this weirdo possibly be me?'

Before her sits the image of a stranger with a semi shaven head and the rainbow shades of a wing shaped top-notch that springs up in spikes from her forehead to the back of her neck. A sprinkling of glitter has been sprayed around the edges.

Bridie thinks of the lunch party. The confident *me* she envisaged had a neat bob highlighted discreetly with a rinse and blow wave. Gwendoline will be consulting her diamond studded watch already and Meredith, the time-keeper of their loose friendship group, will be tut-tutting. She is a stickler for routines, procedures and the rules of etiquette.

Shaken, Bridie sets forth, sweeping past when the gaze of each one of her friends flick over her without recognition. Though they might deny it, in her present guise she is not somebody they might know or wish to know.

All the while she is conscious of the tattooist who stands in the doorway of her shop close by with an amused, but not unkind smile.

'Nice haircut,' she calls.

'Thank you.' Bridie lingers over the display in the tattooist's window, pretending interest, unknowingly taking away one small image above more elaborate works of art. *I've seen that somewhere*, she thinks. *Why that image?* For a split second, she is a child from more than a half century ago, swimming in a freshwater pool with a hundred swallows, dark curves like leaves, dipping and diving all around her. *What happened to the pool and the swallows? What happened to that blissful child?*

Strangely, there is a spring in her step that has been missing lately as she strides unheedingly towards the open area of the shopping mall. The fruit man, usually quite dour, offers her a Sweet Lady apple. He waves a dismissive hand when she offers to pay.

'Nice haircut,' he says, with a grin.

For an insane moment she wants to spread her arms in some kind of sky worship. Above her, beyond the dappled shade of street trees, an endless universe, achingly blue. The bright red apple is sweet. It's white flesh crisp and plump with juice. She sits on a seat near the town library, to eat it, crunching it down to a flimsy core as she and her siblings did as children.

'Nice haircut.' The deep voiced speaker is a regular, seen from a distance on other days. Wheelchair bound; this man likes to doze there under the shade of the trees.

'The haircut? It's a fricking disaster,' she says. 'It's not me at all and not my doing.' She raises her shoulders, as if to absolve herself and then breaks into uncontrolled laughter. 'It's that skunk, Jarrad's fault,' she gasps. 'Kind of, but not really...oh I don't know. Things happen.'

'They do.' The man laughs with Bridie, lighting up a pair of twinkling grey eyes in his deeply lined face. She has seen him there every day, week in, week out, without really seeing him, his smile or the light in his eyes.

'The librarians won't know me. She'll think my card is stolen,' Bridie laments. The wheelchair man grins and offers her his beanie.

'If I need it, I'll let you know,' She can't stop grinning to herself and there it is again, swimming around in her head. That small image. 'I'll give the library a miss today, there's something I must do,' she tells him.

Now here she is with the tattooist hovering over her uncertainly with the needle inches from her face.

'Are you quite sure you want it?' For a full minute the tattooist hesitates. 'I think some of your friends are still waiting, hoping you'll turn up for your lunch date. Well?'

'Please. Just a small one, a swallow with wings spread.' *Like the one on the underside of Marisa's wrist*...is that where it came from? Or was it from another day, another place? Another me?

'Just above your eye?' says the tattooist, 'Or perhaps on the underside of your wrist?'

11 The Good Neighbour

Andy likes things nice. The two shining copper etchings on his high-ceilinged living room wall purchased from a door-to-door salesman a few years ago. The big vase on the corner of the long countertop — one of his many sporting trophies, now filled with a large halo of white lilies. So close to the real thing you wouldn't know the difference. The unblemished gleam of surfaces above a spotless floor.

Smiling, he will escort you round his garden to savour the sweet air. Honey suckle in a pot, clipped back, regular like, before that annoying knot of spent branches spoil the effect. A neat row of tiger lilies standing tall with petunias in the front…and around the islands of neatly clipped shrubbery, you can't go past the old geranium. (He doesn't care that his grown-up kids say they're old fashioned). Much nicer than the low maintenance gardens you see with nothing but fake mulch between hideous cacti and spiky things. Yep. Dead head a geranium regular and Bob's ya uncle.

Andy always dreamed of a couple of palm trees in his front yard and now he has 'em. You just have to keep an eye out for the spent prongs now they are established. Could kill a man easy when they drop, don't you reckon? Bloody things. But it is kind of exciting to have a team of

guys come over to do the lopping. The noise and grand-
ness of the man in the cradle swinging up there with the
wide blue sky behind. A kind of life and death happening
in his own front yard. Then the shiver and shake of the
huge grinding machine in the driveway. He knows the
boss and some of the workers through his sports club.
He and Jillian ask how their mums and dads are going
while they pass around cuppas for a morning break with
freshly made scones, generous slabs of fruit cake, bikkies.
The lot.

A bit of a let-down next day, unless he calls a neighbour over for a cuppa. Andy likes nothing better than to
lay out the cups and get the orders while Jillian does the
rest. Always freshly made cake on offer. Not the shop
stuff in his house. Oh no. Nor from the freezer. Can't
you just taste the difference? *God*, he can pick it from a
mile off.

For Andy, his shining house and neat garden are cosy
as a hug on a cold day. But he likes people too. Likes to
advise the young folk. A good neighbour is Andy. When
Glenis from two doors up is away, looking after grandkids or whatever, he'll keep an eye on poor old
Tom…stuck of all things with microwaved frozen meals
and a woman in aged care to look in on him each day!
Yep. Many is the time when Andy shakes his head over
that one. At such times, when he sees Tom's front room
light flick on, he'll nip in to see that he's okay

'How's me little matey?' he might say, forgetting
somebody told him Tom doesn't really like being called,
'his little matey'. But that isn't gonna stop Andy being a

good neighbour, is it? He's damned if it will.

When new tenants move into the front and back rentals next door, Andy looks on with interest. Everyone is equal in Andy's eyes and he doesn't care if you're the king or whatever, you don't get up yourself.

The new neighbour, Francine, in the back house rental next door makes no secret of the fact that she is a prostitute. The mother of a little girl, Autumn, and boy, Ramble who are taken to an aunt when Francine has a customer over. She's branching out on her own in the daytime hours that suit her, hoping it will work out. At such times you hear the slumberous music of the east wafting above the peppermints.

One day when her aunt is unable to have the children, Francine leaves them in the care of Troy, an easy come, easy go kind of character who has taken over the front rental in the same block.

'You'll have them back at mine by five?' Francine asks, anxiously. 'They're in their beds and asleep by seven sharp every night.

'Yare…yare…yare…no worries,' says Troy.

At eight o'clock a frantic Francine knocks on Andy and Jillian's door. She is hysterical. 'My kids…they should be home. Troy said he'd bring them back at five.' Her hands are shaking.

'Have you eaten today?' While Andy hunts for emergency numbers, Jillian comforts Francine as best she can, preparing a light meal of sandwiches and a pot of tea.

'Should I call the police?' Andy hovers over the house phone.

At this, Francine pales. 'Oh no, not the cops.' She collapses in another fit of anguish, a dark cloud of grief and despair hovering over her, almost visible in its intensity. She gulps down some tea and bites into an egg sandwich in an effort to stop shivering.

Meanwhile, Andy slips over to Troy's house. Just as he suspected the young man's car and dingy are missing. It looks like he's taken the kids out on the water. 'Probably without life jackets, the idiot,' Andy mutters. He hoofs it down to the boat ramp a couple of hundred metres away and sure enough, there is Troy's trailer.

A silvery moon comes out from a cloud and he hears the putt, putt, putt of a two-stroke engine. Andy counts heads – he sees Troy bent over the engine and the two kids huddled together. As it comes into the landing and the motor cuts, their chirping voices are filled with wonder. They've clearly had the time of their lives and will always remember their first ever ride in a boat. The magic of the river. Of waddling brown ducks on shore taking off with a flash of blue green wing tips, then landing on the water to swim in perfect symmetry. On overhanging branches of river gums, sun worshipping cormorants with spread wings catching those last glints of light before it fades. Best of all, the thrill of catching a fish for the first time. Only a fiddler or two, not worth eating. But Troy catches a couple of nice fat bream, showing the pair how you had to wait for this kind of fish while it played with the bait and then on the third strike, you pull it in quickly.

Troy will earn a disapproving look from Jillian and a

severe tongue lashing from Francine, but like the children, he too, has gained a memory; precious in a drug-hazed future in which he will die many times over. It is Andy who saves him more than once. Saves him and his dog, a poor unfortunate beast bought to engage in illegal dog fighting. Armed with a sharp knife in one hand, while Troy is away on one of his mysterious 'jobs', Andy will crawl under Guy's low stumped home to rescue Blue where he is tangled in a rope tethered to the ground.

Weeks pass until, Andy wakens one night in the midst of a heavy sleep. Afterwards, he wonders why. Why did he wake up knowing he needed to go outside, that somebody was in trouble? There is no moon to guide him, just a glimmer from a streetlight that shows him Troy's inert body in the middle of the road. He is in the direct path of a crop of local boys, newly released from school. With beat up cars, their idea of fun is to spin around in the gravel patch near the boat ramp. Then to speed up a rise, past darkened houses on one side with the aim of flattening the orange post that marks the bus stop opposite.

In a drug induced stupor, Troy is unable to grasp the notion that he might be in danger. With the sound of revved up cars and utes close, there is no time to lose. Andy takes a deep breath, pulls Troy into a standing position and heaves him up onto his own back. He staggers across the road to Troy's house only to find both doors locked. Still burdened with the young man's weight, he eyes an old fashioned, unlocked, double sized window that is thankfully low to the ground.

'I got the blighter through,' he will tell Jillian shortly after. Andy is soon fast asleep leaving his wife wide awake.

'My big idiot,' Jillian whispers snuggling into his broad back, then giggles at the thought of Troy waking up on his living room floor, wondering how on earth he got there. Years later, a much older and marginally wiser Troy appears at the door with a couple of 'tinnies' to thank him for, 'Saving my life,' he says.

When Andy succumbs to dementia and dies in his eightieth year, there is standing room only in the funeral parlour with many more spilling into the garden outside. Standing steadfast, is Jillian. 'He was a good man,' she will say. So many will agree with Jillian, who lived in Andy's shadow for so long. But there are compensations.

When Jillian moves that quite heavy vase an inch of so out of place, there is no Andy there to move it right back again. When she replaces the copper etchings on the wall with paintings of her own choosing, there is no Andy to put them right back again. For so long there has only been one way to do anything and that's Andy's way. The right way. As for the rest…she leaves the garden to the kind folk from the Aged Care service. She will offer cake and sometimes scones…bought from the bakery or the Farmer's Market, for she has vowed never to make a fruit cake, a cheesecake, sausage rolls, lamingtons, current slices…ad infinitum, ever again.

12 Seeking Bliss

If Irina told them she came to hear the sound of summer, she might embarrass them – standing on the bank of the river mouth with the tide coming in, lapping faintly against the shore. Wind stirs the stiff leaves of river gums, sings through sheoaks like a choir in some ancient place of worship or in contemplation, nostalgia and longing.

There's a falcon overhead and from far away, the high-pitched cry of its chick. Cicadas beat their mating drums. A sleek black cormorant on the bank gives three deep throated croaks.

Irina enters the river to swim upstream, enclosed in its golden-brown waters. Later, wrapped in a faded beach towel, she returns to the family home among the fruit trees and sprawling garden. The hens are loose. Fat Rhode Island Reds forever changing their ways. From broody, bossy and bullying, to fluffing up their russet feathers in a luxuriant dust bath, pecking happily at a stray sand flea in the feathers of a mate with an itch.

Ben, a kind man who gardens on a Tuesday, has made a little fence to keep the hens from the flowers she planted around the patio. An ex-politician, Irina's unwell husband is a little better today, taking an interest in the veggie patch. He has been watching a parliamentary sitting on TV to see what the buggers are up to. But he worries about the bank balance. The more they have, the more he worries. With his lack of computer skills, this is the first time Irina has been involved with bills and their bank details.

'Can't we do better?' The question hovers when he is uneasy. Once an important manager of people and surrounded by colleagues, he has enjoyed his retirement less and less.

'You were a long time,' he says when she hands him a cup of tea.

'Oh, you missed me, darling,' Irina says with a smile. He looks faintly surprised and embarrassed, but without an answering smile. *Damn her if only she were more predictable and orderly.*

'Penny rang,' he says. 'Their crop is good.'

'Oh, sorry I missed her, I'll call her back.'

'No need.' His mumbled response is interrupted by another call from their daughter. It gets under his skin. He has already told her the wheat crop is a good one. That was about it. So why is she carrying on? The half-heard conversation irritates him. Her repeated words – Yes? And – Really? And those giggles…

He mutters and sighs…letting her know how he feels. How is it she knows more about the children than he does? It annoys him. And she's checking her emails…damn internet ought to be banned. Doing her thing, not worrying about cape weed taking over the lawn. He told her what to do. Easy as you like…to sit on the gardening stool and hook the weed out by the roots with the gardening tool he has made for the job. Change, oh how he hates change.

Meanwhile, Irina senses his negativity like prickles on her skin. The memories slip back. Yesterdays and todays like cards being shuffled. Early morning flights to Canberra when he wakened her by placing his full case on the end of the bed with a thump. Where was he when the children were growing up? And why did he resent her for knowing them so well?

Irena will comfort him when he needs her, as he never could for her, but it doesn't matter. At night she will step outside alone to see the stars. To feel small but full of wonder at the vastness of the unknowable universe and the sheer chance of her own existence. While he sleeps she walks in the early morning as if tethered to the waning moon and rising sun, waiting with intrigued expectation for that first song of a bird and then the chorus.

13 Road's End

'I need Cooper to stay.' A man of few words, Greg really means, *fix it. You owe me. Because our boys have chosen not to be here. Our daughter too.*

I have always believed both Greg and I want to give the best of ourselves to our children. But who can possibly know the what and the why of our offsprings' choices? It isn't a good moment to remind Greg about other farm workers on offer. Strong limbed kids from overseas.

They come with references. Greg fixes their broken cars and I order in goose-fat, dark ryebread and gruesome black sausages. We use Face to Face to speak with their grateful Mor and Far in Denmark. Glimpse into their living rooms awash with family photographs and receive invitations for visits.

Greg wants Cooper to stay. Whether it is a given name or a family name, nobody thought to ask. He came with the flood and no references. He won our hearts.

Hours before the flood and Cooper arrived, our older three kids break their silence. They have come home for the weekend to say goodbye.

'My life is music, says Andrew. 'Music is my life.' Colour drains from his face. 'Accept it, Dad. Mum. Accept me. I'm going to Sydney with my band.'

'And…and…I'm going with him.' Thomas speaks with care, but his hands, so like his dads, are trembling. 'I'm sculpting full time, with a contract for a street art thing in Sydney.' He holds his breath then shouts, 'Jees, Dad, don't you get it?'

'I get that suddenly you're all clearing out.' Red faced and angry, Greg is close to tears.

'I'll be here for you Dad…I don't want to go away to that posh school where I won't know anyone.' Rachel puts her arms around him but he brushes her away.

'So, what about you, Eleanor?' He glares at our eldest. His pride and joy.

'I have a job with a law firm in London and I want to be with Eliot.' Silence and then, 'You and Mum can visit…it's not like I'm dying.'

Greg swings around towards me and is right in my face. Are you happy now?'

I want to scream at him. *Don't ruin what we have*, but he's through the door.

'At heel,' he yells at Gruff and the dog trots after him. Carolling magpies around the backdoor, scatter. Head down, Greg strides across the yard to his workshop. His refuge and temple.

You're a craftsman, I think. Not a farmer. It's just that nobody ever told you.

'Me come too, Daddy?' Little Timmy's face puckers. 'Want Daddy…'

'It's okay, little brother.' Eleanor picks him up. 'Will you come visit me in London?' Her comforting words hang in the air. A gust of wind shakes the window and the old farmhouse judders.

Thomas checks his iPhone. 'There's a storm coming. A big one. Better tell Dad, miserable old bugger.'

All night long, it rattles the windows and knocks at the door. We two lie awake with nothing resolved, while Timmy snuggles in between us. Amidst the howling wind and rain, Rachel crawls into the bottom of our bed. She's been busy with her high beamed torch and is able to tell us the old mulberry tree has fallen, the cubby too.

'You made that cubby for us, Dad,' Rachel murmurs. Uneasily, I doze with a dreadful fear lurking in my gut. Somewhere there's water gushing where no water should be, and that tick, tick, ticking sound that comes with a flood.

I wake up screaming his name. 'Timmy.' Where is Timmy? All of us are still in our night clothes, out of the house heading down the slope. Before us it swirls, a great stretch of water that our fearless Timmy has never experienced. To our children, raised in dry dock, it is jokingly called the big-drink. Usually it's a trickle on a poorly drained road, but now it's a full-blown river lapping at the land between its banks. Frantic searching in that dreadful space, no parent wishes to go, and then he comes. Cooper, exhausted and shivering. Comes with our Timmy in his arms. The darling of our hearts. Water streams from his small nose and mouth, but his breathing comes in big, beautiful gulps.

Nobody thinks to call him anything but Cooper. Our Timmy believes he and Cooper can breathe under water. Didn't they see leaves and sticks floating like fish? And Cooper's arms reaching for him? Timmy knows right away, Cooper is there to bring him home. At fifteen,

Rachel is already in love with him and Greg can't do with-out a co-worker who can think for himself. Now I am supposed to be the one who persuades him to stay, to be registered as staff.

Like Cooper, I came to Road's End without a refer-ence. Nearly came to grief on that patch of poorly drained road in the creek bed. I remember, the sense of homecoming as I sighted the rambling farmhouse with its wrap-around veranda tucked into the slope. Gnarly old fruit trees, bare on a winter's day but still offering apples, yellow and delicious. And that irresistible grey-green sea of a bush reserve that marks the road's end. Oh yes, I too, came without a reference.

Greg fixed my battered car. Fixed it neat. Four near new tyres from his collection. Dents smoothed out. On that day so long ago, I take in the silence of his workshop. The peace and sureness of his pace. He looks deeply into my eyes and I drown in the calm of his. Is it too late to find that person I saw and loved all those years ago? But now for Cooper. Do I really think he should stay?

When Cooper handed back our son, I saw in his eyes an expression I will not forget. And now it is there in his eyes again. He will tell me his story and why he must leave. He knows and I know, I will keep it to myself. Sea-sons have passed since I found the prison greens on the bank and buried them. Buried them deep. No matter what others might say when he hands himself in, for us, our Timmy is his reference and it will always be good enough for me.

'That's good…I saved him,' Cooper says, 'but that lit-tle boy…he saved me.'

14 Taking Lucy Home

They could like it or not. 'I'm taking Lucy home.'

The light was still strong when David moved away from the outside setting where Trudy was serving iced tea. He couldn't stay a minute longer with his blood pressure rising and Tom sitting across from him, shaking his head, dumbstruck by David's words.

'Does she still know you, David?' This from Trudy, in careful hushed tones.

'She knows me.'

After kicking up a stink at the hospital he was still flustered and defensive. He had found her, half in, half out, of a hopelessly inadequate chair with her head and neck awkwardly curved towards her chest and slipping. On the trolley beside her was a cup of cold tea and a stale, uneaten meal. The thought of it made him angry all over again. He picked up the hat she'd bought for him only last summer, and then left. It was pointless to stay, pointless to say anything more to his brother and Trudy.

Before he was out of sight but still within earshot, Tom was already muttering, calling him a stubborn, self-defeating bugger.

'But he wants to take her home,' Trudy said, in a pained way. He really *wants to take her home.*'

'Don't you dare encourage him,' Tom said.

'I only wish I had. I feel so ashamed.' Trudy wept.

David drove towards his farm full of savagery. The speeding ute wobbled. He veered off the gravel road, skidded, then self-corrected, but he was shivering all over. He might have been thirty again, crawling out of his rolled car in this same spot after his parting row with Vanessa. How that woman had hurt him, yet the anguish he felt, seemed remote and futile now. As though it had happened to somebody else.

Still shivering, he pulled up at a parking bay. It was tucked behind a stand of big tuart trees along with peppermints and a scruffy old jarrah gawking into the sky. He climbed out of the vehicle and leaned against the cab, trying to block stupid tears that sprang from a deep well of sorrow that had been building inside him. He heard his own sobs, as cranky and hoarse as a rusty old windmill.

'I'm not good at crying,' he mumbled to the ants around his feet.

The unheeding wind ruffled the trees. Birds went on warbling, chattering, squawking. After a while he recovered his equanimity. Through wet eyes he took in his surroundings. He and Lucy had stopped here once to feed Catherine, their newly adopted daughter, blue eyed, beautiful. He hadn't known a baby's cry could be so loud, so lustful and hungry. He laughed, remembering his irrational fear that her desperate cries were not 'normal'.

As if Aunt Eleanor's dire warnings about 'bad blood' had finally struck home. The adoption issue was only one of the irritations to which Lucy had been subjected when she came to live on their sprawling cross-generational family property in the southwest.

David's churning mind flung snapshots of their life in his face. He thought of the foolish beliefs that could hold you back, the outdated wisdoms that could defeat you before you even started. And his own personal baggage, Vanessa, a shining bubble, an itch under his skin. Within her persona, the perception of an elusive, never to be found 'something' for which he once longed.

When he met Lucy, David still had the bitter aftertaste of failure on his tongue. The date was arranged by Tom. David went along with it just to shut him up. Trudy's friend Lucy needed a partner for the Annual Show Ball, and really, David 'old boy', you wouldn't have to do any-thing. Just be there. He didn't even have to take the girl home.

'But, I'm taking the girl home,' David finally re-sponded, grinning. Back in the fifties, it was part of the ritual, the conniving and courting, the licet and illicit love making, all leading to one or other thing: right or wrong, marriage or desertion, with no in-betweens.

Funny, come to think of it. Side-splitting, belly aching, laugh-a minute funny. So why am I crying? Silly old coot. If he concentrated, David could visualize Lucy as she was then, a petite little thing with a tiny waist walking through the foyer of the Manji pub. Her dress was pale green made of shiny fabric that rustled as she walked. Her fair hair fell in a glossy 'page boy' around her face. She wasn't strictly 'pretty' yet everything about her was pretty, her feet, her hands and the way she moved. When she spoke, her voice was surprisingly firm, resonant. Her intelligent eyes, direct and kind. She would never shame him. She would never flirt brazenly with other men or make him feel like a fool.

Yet later when she took his arm to dance a sedate Pride of Erin, he wanted to walk away without explanation. He forced himself on to the dance floor, his rangy frame wooden, unbending. He could hear the words in his head but he couldn't feel the music. *I'm forever blowing bubbles, pretty bubbles in the air…*

'Feeling lonely up there?' Lucy smiled impishly, her eyes full of warmth and light. He couldn't look away. They recovered the glitch, and he listened for the beat, allowing the music to seep into him as they moved into the waltz sequence of the dance.

Funny how people grow on you; funny how he came to rely on her. Apart from an occasional duty-dance with Trudy, he only ever danced with Lucy. Before they married, there was one lapse into restlessness. For a few miserable weeks they parted and then he saw her again and they literally fell into each other's arms. Afterwards he wondered why he put them through such pain.

Stupid, stupid, stupid. He should have known it had already been decided on that first night with that first look that told him, I accept you. I want to be with you. What more does anyone need? It was like the coming of a season. How could you not flow with the season? She became his wife, his lover, his co-worker, share-farmer, business adviser. They mourned failed pregnancies and their stillborn child together, celebrated their adopted daughter's graduation in nursing, their adopted son's brilliance in medical research. They shared in the pride and sense of loss when Catherine and Toby left home to lead their own lives.

They were planning a much-awaited holiday adventure with Tom and Trudy when he noticed her first lapse of memory, something as funny and simple as feeding their over-fat hens three times in a day. They laughed over it with the afternoon light golden, slanting in on the backyard, casting beams of light over Lucy's garden. So many seasons of planning.

The light is fading now and it is time for us to leave him. David, the beloved, and Lucy. The wind gusts through the stand of trees. The tall, rangy farmer is small beneath them as the branches and leaves set up a low murmur of dissent. Not against him, I fancy but for him, increasing in strength, strong in their opposition to the voices of well-meaning loved ones and those of the health professionals trying to dissuade him. I hear his voice, creaky and low as he calls out, 'To hell with you.' The trees sough again and his voice rises, grows stronger and clearer, as he sends his message into the night: 'I said to hell with you. I'm taking Lucy home.'[1]

---

[1] First published in "Woorilla" literary magazine, Vol 16 No.1, 2007.

15 Everything is Fine

Thomas, the man in Room 12 is worried that he has forgotten something important.

'Did I fill the ute with petrol?' he might ask. He's afraid his wife, Lena and daughter, Dee, are stuck on the road somewhere. The details are a jumble. Half dream. Half heard conversations.

Is Marie, his second born daughter here? His anxiety grows until he is distracted by the sheer effort of everyday living. Of eating and drinking sweet, thickened tea from a weird spouted object. Where is his favourite cup? He wants to stand up and do a proper pee. The gentle Irish nurse calls him, "Sweetie", then there is the other one with consonances sharp as tacks and vowels full of tension. He thinks Lena is here, then not here, when in fact the converse is true, for God's sake.

'I'm here,' she tells him firmly in a voice he can't deny.

Has she been here all the time?

'Damn it, damn it. I forgot to fill the tank…you were stuck,' he mutters.

She holds his hand tightly. 'Everything is fine.'

For Lena, it is still something of a shock to see the bed clothes sag where his fine boned legs should be. He'd been a strider, an athlete. She pictures them holding him steady in his boat, while hauling in a big snapper. The sky a hard blue, the sea darker again, white tipped, silver streaks of sunlight dancing.

'You were stuck…I should have…'

'It is quite okay.'

Is it his intuition, she wonders, that he guessed something was amiss? Tears well in her eyes. That he still has the impulse to look out for his family.

'Marie is here.'

He nods.

Their daughter, Marie has come, part way by train to the rail terminal a hundred K's away. The plan had been for Dee to meet her, but after filling her car with petrol she became seriously unwell.

'I think it's the ear infection,' Dee said. 'Mum, I can't possibly drive like this.'

'You rest. I'll be fine driving mine.'

Lena recalls the crunch of the Holden's wheels over the gravel driveway and then spinning through the suburbs to the highway – a black ribbon winding through forest and farmland. And her inner being, shedding the shawl of exhaustion yet again. Now just this task and nothing more. A sense of pending disaster and darkness that has hovered for days slips away. *Look at the glimmer of light in the silvery winter sky.*

'Oh yes,' she tells him, breath heaving from the rush. 'Marie will be here to see you in a moment.'

'And the others?'

'All fine…everything is fine.'

16 The Gun

You think I'm afraid? The Ex-soldier? Of course, I'm afraid. It's like stepping up on stage. Afraid is everything. To be treasured like gold or a good vintage red. With steady hands, I pull it out of the drawer. A sleek piece of work. A bargain at a hundred and eighty bucks. Skinny barrelled — long, like me. A Feinwerkbau. Model 65, reference Q 128. Action — side lever. Single shot. Barrel length 196 cm. Powerful.

When you come with the boy as you promised all will be as it should. My darling, do you remember the good times? Do you remember our great plan to make a self-sustaining garden? That was before…before the darkness. Before the nightmare consumed us. You call it self-doubt and then an illness. But I never doubted. I hate to say this but it is your madness. Not mine. Your madness when you lost belief in me. When you colluded with the do-gooders and our so-called school friend, "Doctor" Brad. The fool. Just a farm kid like me full of book learning who worked the system. No cleverer than I. You said so yourself.

I forgive you for your lapse. Of course, I forgive you. Now that you've come to your senses. I can tell you. It was Brad who spread the rumour…said you gave up on friendships because of your pride. That you tried to keep up the illusion of a perfect family. It makes me wild. As if we should tell everyone our business…wear our hearts on our sleeves. Spread it all over the internet? We don't do that sort of thing and that's why I insisted on home schooling for the boy. You, me and the boy. We stick together. We are one. Complete in ourselves. You are a counsellor, for God's sake. You take care of the weak broken ones. We are not broken. Brad and his ilk are the ones who are broken. I am you and you are me and our child is part of us. If one goes, we all go. One, two, three. There'll be no separation. One dies and we all die. Anything else is unthinkable.

When the time comes, please don't argue. Read me. Read my eyes and you'll see this is the way it must be. You'll agree, I've chosen the right place for an ending. This third-generation farm was the beginning, you see. It is like closing a circle. Neat like this gun.

I listen for the creaks and murmurs of the old house with its roughly hewn walls and pressed tin ceilings. You will see the fire I have made. Built with care from the bush kindling and those mallee roots we picked from your uncle's farm. See how I graded them by size? Neat. Maybe you'll agree to sit a while. As a kid, I would sit here without a lamp. Curled up in the old Morris chair.

I loosen my hold on the gun, rest my elbows on the sheoak arms of the chair and simply look. I love the crackle and flare of a new fire, and then that soft first heat which has a sound of its own. Muted. Subtle. Yellow, blue and red, the flames leap and devour. But before the slow burning wood turns to fine white ash, it becomes a mini palace of gold. My love, my first and only love, didn't we have such a moment?

I stretch my legs towards the fire, suddenly drowsy. The realisation is a trigger for that leg of mine. The jumping nerve that has a mind of its own. This is no time to fall asleep, man, I tell myself, though I haven't slept…not properly, for days. I tighten my hand on the gun. Its lines are clean. Its mechanism simple. Neat. Almost virginal you might say. Beautiful with the firelight reflected on its surfaces. It has never been used to kill a person, I'm told. It came from a guy in a gun club. They shoot at dummy targets. Can you believe such a place exists? Stupid. That kind are not for you and me. You, me and our boy.

Do you know? My fear has dissipated in the old place and I'm feeling refreshed. Brave enough to face an ending. It will not be pretty. I know that. A blood bath…I see the headlines. Weird that for all my careful planning, there are other endings that begin to play like the shorts of a movie flicking through my head. People want happy endings, you see. Happy endings that raise their spirits and give them false hope.

Woman and boy escape death — speak of their desperate flight through dense scrub before reaching the township and safety. Boy tells harrowing story — I hear Dad's sick voice and I run to my special place near the old well. Family friend — town's GP Doctor Brad Stewart local Doctor stops a blood bath.

My head is fuzzy with unwanted images. I see the sensitive faces, one like the other. You and my boy stricken with grief. Suddenly I want to scream at you, *Run. For God's sake run. Away from me. Run for your lives and don't turn back.*

My grip tightens on the gun. I step out on to the veranda, using the torch on my mobile. The old veranda creaks under my feet and then I'm wading through dew drenched grass as I head for the old well and now I hear the distant sound of a vehicle. So, you are coming just as you promised? My heart begins to race. I carry on towards the well and lean the gun against the pepper tree where the boy likes to hide even though he doesn't know I know. 'It's too close to the well.' So often I would tell him.

I try to prise off the cover. Heavy jarrah boards, laden with clumps of paspalum grass that cling and grasp. With wheezy grunts I lift one heavy jarrah sleeper, pulling it away from the tangled grass and compacted clay soil. And then another. A glimpse of dark water and I take in an earthy smell…tainted not with something dead, but something old as time. My skin prickles and then, like some kind of robotic likeness of a man, I pick up the Feinwerkbau and drop it, barrel first, into the space. It lands sideways with a gurgling rush. My phone torch shows it sinking. Disappearing in a spring of bubbles. I turn back, clumsily stabbing at the phone expecting to see your number, but its Brad, five times over in a list of missed calls.

From across the paddocks I watch the lights of his four-wheel drive speeding towards the house. He screeches to a stop and you are out of the passenger's side of his car yelling my name. Brad is behind you and I glimpse our son sitting in the back seat. Rod like. His face a taut pale blur in the dim light.

Something between a sob and a cry pushes against my throat. I'm trying to tell my love I drowned something that cost us $180 and it was a fool of an idea. I want to tell her I'm sorry and to please forgive me. It comes with gut wrenching nausea and my tear ducts grotesque and swelling. Like an earthen dam, holding back a raging flood so fierce it might surely wipe out our livelihood, our innocence and our dreams.

17 The Letter

It is a fat letter loaded with papers, delivered by courier. Not good news but strangely, it lifts the veil of depression and loneliness — a dark space in which Linley beats herself up in self-imposed isolation. The simple act of receiving a letter…a big deal? How pathetic is that?

From his hand to hers. The courier is a real live human being with blood flowing in his veins like hers. Breathing the same air. Bitterly cold, bracing, or gently warm in turn, it has been a month since Linley fronted up to the supermarket to top up her meagre supplies. A smile and a nod to and from the supervisor at the self-service checkout is the nearest she has come to a real-life person in a long time.

The courier is a middle-aged man with tired eyes like her own. She wonders if he guesses she is a self-imposed isolate, and that sometimes out of sheer loneliness, she will speak her deepest sorrows to a stranger. And then, ashamed, will retreat to her cave – that shabby holiday house with an unloved garden in the outer suburb to which she is tethered. If she listens carefully after the traffic sounds have abated, she might just hear the sound of the sea.

Sometimes she will look with longing when she sees a young mother and child, though she has never given birth herself. Too afraid. To impose herself on an innocent is unthinkable. Her husband called her condition agoraphobia. Claimed he loved her but couldn't live with *it*. For that reason, she moved out of their jointly owned house and place of business. The courier is close to her own height and so when his gaze meets hers, she sees the depth of his grey green eyes. A calm sea. He reads her too well.

'Sign. Just sign here.' He seems impatient now, wanting to be done with her. She scribbles her name with his cumbersome electric gadget, and having handed her the well-sealed letter, she expects him to leave at once.

Vaguely uncomfortable at his continued presence she asks, 'Why…why are you still here?'

For just a shade too long, he says nothing and then — 'To be honest, I think I should stay until you open your letter.'

'Why would you do that?' She speaks more sharply than she means to. Her upbringing tells her his words are highly inappropriate but she is strangely moved.

'Whatever is in that letter, good news or bad,' he says, 'You need to share the pain or the joy with somebody.' The smile not on his lips but in his eyes. Eyes like the sea. Truly the kindest she ever saw. Ah, the sea…calm or wild, she has always loved it. So why? *Why have I deprived myself of the place I love so well?* Images flick through her mind - the regular roar and rush, the hush of a wave…bare feet in sand…arms outstretched…counting ships on the far horizon. Waves coming in and out. Like a regular breath. Trustworthy and predictable.

I must go down to the sea, a poet once said. Her own mother, in the last pain ridden days of her life, mistaking the air conditioner of the Fremantle hospital for the sea air. Perhaps the sound of the Indian Ocean's endless rhythm had penetrated its walls to offer her comfort.

Linley asks herself, why have I stayed away so long? Away from the sea and the people I love. Sisters, brothers, their wives and children. Nieces and nephews growing so quickly from early childhood into gawky teenagers tentatively voicing their ideas. Where are they now? She wonders. Is it too late? Have they given up on her too?

The courier man tells her about his pet gecko, how he lets it into his house for a visit. After he feeds it strawberries, the strange reptilian leaves through the open flywire door with a faint nod as if to say, 'Thank you, kind sir.' The courier tells her about a family of mice under his house who obligingly eat his left-over cheese, and his bird bath filled with fresh water each day for the squabbling parrots. This man lives alone but she senses that he is rarely lonely. He works for some charity as a financial adviser.

Linley is conscious of his eyes on her as she opens the letter, facing the startling facts she has so carefully avoided for so long. *I am still breathing,* she thinks…*I will go on breathing.* Of course, her husband…must marry his new love. Make a home and have children. Though he promises not to leave her destitute, he would like her to give up the jointly owned holiday cottage where she now lives. Of course, there will be a payout. His words are not cruel, but echo with shades of his steely core. He seems to have forgotten it was her inheritance that allowed him to set up his business and home. But he loves to bargain and he loves to win. *Not this time.*

Linley looks at the windows of the cottage with fresh eyes, the long windows that let in soft nurturing light, even on her bad days. With a new surge of energy rising, she resolves to clean those windows of accumulated dust and cobwebs. She resolves to plant a garden. A lemon and a pomegranate. Cineraria for their rich colour and stocks for their perfume. She will fill the veggie beds with nutrients and attend the poor neglected herbs with their wonderful healing attributes.

'Are you…Are you okay?' the Courier asks.

'I am.' She smiles, holding back a flood of emotion for she has made one whole decision, the first in a long, long time. 'I am…I will be…okay.'

As for that letter with its accompanying forms for her to fill in? A signal for her to succumb to another will like always? The Courier watches while she tears those offending pages into small bits and drops them in the wheelie bin on the kerb. They turn to each other and they smile.

18 Consolation

As I drive into the nursing home car park, for a split second I am blinded by the flash of sunlight in my eyes. I stop and get a toot from behind by an impatient driver. He revs his powerful engine and with a rude finger sign, shoots past me. Shaken, I find a parking spot and sit for a time, wanting to restore my equanimity before spending the day with my disabled husband. There's a story from my childhood resounding in my head.

I was perhaps nine or ten. My mother and we children were visiting an old family friend — Mrs Simms, who was basking in the joy of a visit from her newly married daughter, Tricia and her husband, Andrew. The couple had arrived the night before and were in fine form, laughing and teasing each other, romping around like children. I recall the sheen of Tricia's long black hair, the white of her teeth as she laughed with mouth open when he tickled her. Andrew was a smallish man, but athletic and strong as he curved her into the arc of his arms. The idea of arms around me like that warmed me. It was my first impression of young love, an awakening of sorts, but I was also conscious of my mother's joy in it. For that reason, I was puzzled when her eyes brimmed with tears. I sensed, but was too young to realise, that for her, the couple's happiness symbolised her faith in the human capacity to recover from trauma.

It came to me later with a story told in hushed tones. Andrew had been married to Katherine, his present wife's sister. They had taken up an abandoned property, with the idea of acquiring it one day. Meanwhile there was plenty of work for a capable accountant like Andrew. He could work from home but also use his motorcycle to meet with customers in the township, some seven miles away.

For Katherine, Saturday mornings were special shopping days but also a time for catching up with family and friends. I remember those days myself. The mixed-up smells of the grocery store with the lady of the household reading out each item on her shopping list and Edith, one of the serving girls, fetching each one to be placed in a cardboard box. Money paid was placed in a small container and sent to the store's accountant on an elaborate conveyer belt overhead with a whirring and tinging of electronic gadgetry. It was all part of the excitement of a Saturday morning in our country town.

Nobody seemed to mind waiting, it was the modern-day equivalent of a big family party. Later, Katherine and Andrew might choose to have a three-course meal at the tearooms or to enjoy the novelty of fish and chips served with a little salad at the café by the handsome Greek owner. With all this to look forward to, Katherine climbed aboard the motorcycle, dressed in her best finery, nestling happily into Andrew's back.

They were soon on the winding gravel road with

overhanging trees on both sides. As they approached a moderately steep rise with the glaring sun behind, Andrew saw the massive black shape of a truck bearing down on them. The truck driver momentarily blinded by the flash from the glaring sun could do nothing before the crash.

Andrew came to his senses with unbearable pain in his shoulder and hip, the smell of hot metal and above all, the sound of Katherine's breathing. A moan, yet not a moan at all…but lungs gasping for life, the inward and the outward breath. In and out. In and out. And then silence. It took weeks and weeks for the grieving young husband to recover. With his own family far away, it was Katherine's family who were there to support and nurture him and Tricia who showed him it was possible to love again.

It is a story that has never quite left me. I realise this, as I wend my way into the nursing home – back to my own story with a sense of time…indifferent time flickering. For each of us, the joys and sorrows of its passing.

19 Darina - Myth Maker

After her visit to mine, and mine to Darina's, I sigh with relief as I go outside to sit under the patio at home. I close my eyes and take in sounds: an orchestra of bird song, the drone of a plane — somebody doing his or her flying time? From far away the muted roar of traffic. I like to imagine it is the ocean rolling in and out with those glorious pauses in between.

I can't help but relish my peaceful household. How I need it after three disturbing days when I entertained my friend — a close friend from our nursing days. At seventeen we nursed at a private hospital before being called up by a leading hospital to train as qualified nurses. Darina and I are also connected by family knowledge and friendships.

We have been separated all our married lives, with perhaps one or two meetings in between, but we are always happy to see each other. It's a kind of unconditional affection we share, but oh, what hard work! On this last visit, Darina searches my fridge for 'something to give her a lift'. I offer her tea, coffee or even milk, but she makes do with some left-over table wine of doubtful vintage. The next day, I take her home and stay overnight. She is with her aging husband, a once successful businessman who suffers from slight dementia. Also there, a fine-looking but troubled son in his middle years who looks out for his parents. Darina's family story is the unhappy reversal of a rags to riches tale, with the loss of a fine house in a fine suburb.

How can I explain my mixed feelings of affection, irritation and bewilderment as I realise my friend is not only addicted to alcohol but also a compulsive collector of tragic tales? While I negotiate city traffic, becoming vaguely lost along the way, she cross-examines me about family events of which she knows little but the bare outlines. She digs for fine detail like a hound after truffles.

'You should have worked for the damn tabloid press,' I mutter, as she gasps over some titbit I have given her while distracted by the sight of the turn-off to her home flashing by. The story I've given away will make fine fodder for inference and wild speculations by my friend. Like a magnet, she is drawn where the heavy hand of fate hits hardest, especially when the consequences expose extremes of human weakness and/or heroism.

But isn't this what all story tellers do? I ask myself, irritably, as she crosses herself yet again. It is a distracting habit she has developed since her conversion to Catholicism. Perhaps in unconscious rivalry with a mutual close friend who regularly calls on, 'Our Lord' for counsel while rescuing Darina from her latest scrape (like being stranded in her car miles from anywhere because she is too drunk to drive).

You're an oral storyteller, though you don't know it, I decide. You do what story tellers do. It is what writers do. But for Darina it is life itself. Early deaths, accidents, any hint of public disgrace and equally the slightest hint of cleverness, wealth or notoriety go into the mix and a Darina myth is born. In a long-ago life she might have been a famous medicine woman, adviser, and moral guide. She has a knack for fostering a kind of intimacy with others that endears people from all walks of life and of course she knows all of their stories.

That brings me to Darina's background; to the women who were most influential. Generous hearted homemakers, gardeners, cooks, providers of food and daily comfort to their families from a rural setting of small townships and tight knit communities. Darina has that same generosity of spirit and flare for homemaking. Her feeling for style has been enhanced by becoming the respected leader in her field and living the good life in a wealthy suburb of a city.

As for the passion with which she tells her tales; her aunt was among the first to sign up to be 'saved' by Billy Graham and gravitated towards a community of believers. In a similar way, Darina is attracted to the ritual and richness of the Roman Catholic Church. She converted in midlife and seemed to revel in being part of a prestigious congregation of Catholics. Now that she is separated from that parish she feels 'humiliated' to use her own words. It's as if the whole basis of her belief system has been shattered by the change in suburbs.

The need to tell our stories has come full circle. An image comes to mind of Darina's grandmother, a small round woman with fair skin and sky-blue eyes. In the light of an open fireplace her snow-white hair is close to my mother's dark head of hair as they whisper together.

'She is sound asleep', my mother says, as she tucks a

blanket around my shoulders on the couch beside her. I lie perfectly still. I am about nine, awake and all ears as I hear a story way beyond my years, an absorbing tale of wickedness and reprisal whispered in the best oral tradition from the lips of Darina's grandmother. My mother also has more than a tale or two to tell.

Back to the present. With typical generosity, Darina gives up her bed for me while retiring to 'Lily's bed' that is set up as a kind of memorial to her much beloved late sister. She is the subject of the last story of the day, one that is full of pathos and touching sisterly love. But I smile as she falls into a blissful sleep between the two over indulged poodles that share 'Lily's' bed.

I am often discomforted by Darina's slanted conclusions on the slim evidence of hearsay, but I shrug. 'That's just Darina,' I will tell myself. Yet underneath I am deeply disturbed by her present vulnerability. I am sad for the family of my friend and for Darina who unheedingly orchestrates her own living drama – a story that seems truly tragic with only one end in sight. I mourn for the loss of certainty about one's identity and place in the community and the world. For Darina and other vulnerable souls, it can become an Achilles heel that is the stuff of true tragedy.

A year or two went by before I attended her funeral, 'down south' as they say. She had been well cared for after her husband's death and reconciled with a beloved daughter and a spread of grandchildren who speak with joy of holidays spent with that fun-loving rascal with whom I shared an important part of my girlhood.

20 Perfection

I am a ten-year-old boy, just a couple of centimetres shorter than my nan. It is Saturday morning and we are planning to go to a family wedding on Sunday. It is to be held in a garden on the foreshore of the Swan. Mum is doing the catering and after setting up the business all by herself, expects…well…nothing short of perfection. When she drops us off at Dad's house, she gives him strict instructions to dress us in our best.

'Sara must wear her flowery sundress, and her white shoes,' Mum says.

'And for me?' I ask.

'Your cream shirt, but Dad will need to buy you a nice pair of brown dress shorts with a leather belt.' She mentions the shop where she has seen the shorts advertised. 'Remember to tuck in your shirt,' she adds.

'Ugh,' I mutter darkly. The truth is, I do not want brown shorts or new shorts at all. I vow to stick to my comfy old school shorts if there's nothing else in my wardrobe that still fits me, and I do — this is how I manage it.

When dad takes me shopping I try on the brown shorts while cunningly leaving my old school pants underneath. When I emerge from the fitting room, Dad frowns. Shakes his head looking puzzled.

'They are not okay, Dad,' I mumble.

'They do look kind of bulky and weird.' He checks his watch and with a nonchalant shrug, agrees that the old shorts look much better.

'Let's go home, then.' As usual, he has a heap of jobs waiting and soon forgets the issue completely.

In the morning when we climb into the four-wheel drive to go to the wedding, l wish I had new shorts because my old ones don't look right, especially with the cream shirt tucked in. In a last-minute desperate act, Dad has cut down one of his old belts to fit me, (Mum has told me to tuck in my shirt and wear a belt and so a belt it must be).

'I don't want to go,' I mutter. 'There'll be a million rellies I hardly know.'

'Not quite a million,' Dad laughs. 'You'll be okay.'

Meanwhile, my sister talks over me (I reckon it is her new extension class encouraging her to speak up about everything under the sun…damn silly idea in my view). She is going on about the daytime moon we had noticed in the sky earlier.

'There's a rabbit in the moon,' she says.

'Don't be silly,' I sneer.

Her voice rises. 'Yes, I tell you there's a rabbit in the moon and Neil Armstrong saw it…it's on the internet and it's true.'

I give her the 'look', rolling my eyes and this makes her mad (just as I predicted).

'There's a rabbit on the moon…you can see its ears,' she says in a high-pitched screech.

'There are craters on the moon,' I say. 'Rocks and dust.' Before long we are both yelling and Dad is yelling at us to please shut up. Normally he might remind me that my sister is almost three years younger than I. But today he's trying to get on the freeway and then fairly soon, he needs to shoot off the freeway into South Perth and if we keep fighting, he'll end up in Timbuktu or the South Pole.

It's as hot as hades when we hunt for a spot to park. As soon as we find it, I nod to my sister. 'Race?' Our mutually agreed signal to take off — each of us wanting to be the first to sight Mum. Dad calls after us of course, afraid we'll be lost, kidnapped, run over or whatever. We slow down when we see Mum's van and all her stuff. There, under the shade of trees are trestles laden with dish after dish. We stand there with eyes big, our bellies empty and mouths watering.

'Does it look okay?' Mum asks.

'Hell yes,' Dad says, coming up behind us, sweating a bit from chasing us. There's soft music playing from the sound system already in place. Big platters lined with edible leaves are heaped up with fruity smelling fruit. There are fresh bready smelling breads, creamy yoghurts and Mum's delicious spicy fries.

The rellies are gathering, all dressed up. I'm getting hugs from aunties and uncles. I'm a bit shy with faces I don't know but it's weird because they look ridiculously familiar. I meet a boy a bit older than me. Turns out he's a second cousin. He is bilingual because his mum comes from Japan. We like the same music and games. My sister is running around with some other second or even third cousins. She's taken off her shoes and tucked in her dress, somehow, to climb a big sprawling tree.

The bride and groom will come after a church ceremony…and we aren't allowed to eat until then. Fair enough, I suppose, so we are doubly pleased when they appear. The groom is my dad's cousin and he's wearing a pale grey suit, white dress shirt and the biggest smile in the world on his face. His bride is smiling too. She's wearing something wispy and white. A veil that is kind of floaty like those little white clouds in the sky. And like the clouds, the morning floats away from us without our knowing. Before we leave with Dad, Mum hugs us. She doesn't say a word about my shorts or my sister's bare feet. Afterwards, dad takes us for a swim at City Beach to cool off. He shows us when and how to catch a wave with our new surf boards. My sister and I laugh our heads off. We forget all about the moon argument. PS: I forgot to tell you, everyone loved Mum's wedding feast and I agree, it was…perfect.

21 The Wayside Pub and Air Surfing

The Wayside pub is a welcome surprise after farm and bushland. A double gabled conglomerate in brick, iron and jarrah, softened by time yet full of warmth. Still redolent with the state's history. Beyond — you will see a smattering of well-worn timber homes with gardens and fruit trees hanging over fences — the residents make up the pub's clientele for the most part. Old folk and the sports loving young when their matches are at home.

Greg Harris, who has taken over the lease of the pub has joined the footy club and put his name down for coaching young players in netball. The locals already love him. Oh yes, they do, thinks Jillian with a rueful half-smile. Her big handsome husband with those keen brown eyes and white toothed smile, but most of all, his eternal optimism. A kind of lovable innocence.

She hears him greeting customers as they arrive. 'Hello, there. Oh Sharon, you're looking gorgeous in that dress…you're one of those women who can wear red…Gordon, how are you, mate? Great tennis this morning! You sure know how to smash 'em.

Jillian slices through a pile of ham sandwiches and reminds herself to check on the sausage rolls; Greg's idea to encourage the locals. Heaven knows, with a bank balance running on empty, they need the trade. She learned of Greg's decision to take on the lease of the pub after the fact, but through a habit of a lifetime, holds her tongue. It doesn't stop her worrying about their future. Their son, Steen who has just finished an apprenticeship in electronics, offered to help out until the place was 'on its feet'. Would that ever happen?

'But Mum, what about your half-made retirement house near the beach?' He worried on her behalf.

'Dad said…we'll get the builders working again…just as soon as—'

'Heard that one before,' he says. Now as they squeeze past each other, she notices a worried frown between his eyes. Steen was not tall like his dad. Just average in height and fine boned.

'Do you hear that noise…is it a storm?'

'Yeah…I hear it.'

Jillian steps outside. A whirly wind is picking up bits of dry fallen leaves in the parking area, but that isn't it. Two crows float above her, making small un-crow-like sounds. The female coming from behind, suddenly turns from her partner to float on her back. The male darts in an upward sweep, hanging there like a question mark in the quivering air, looking down as if surprised at his mate's wilful display of independence. Then comes an unmistakable roar.

The bikies have come to town. Wearing the signature of the 'Jays' they roll into the parking lot with clouds of dust in their wake, then stand, row after row, like warriors beside armed chariots waiting for something to happen. Jillian hot foots it back to her sandwich making. She glances at Greg whose brown eyes flicker with alarm. Greg is a fine figure of a man himself, but not as big as the Jay's leader, who strides into the Wayside, with the confidence of a tried-and-true leader of men.

'Call me Blackbutt,' he says. A giant with massive limbs and a strangely compelling gaze. Gold tinted tree serpent tattoos on either side of his face lead to the central points, his eyes, a mixture of pale blue and grey, flecked with green. Greg swallows a lump of fear in his belly, squaring his shoulders. He forces a smile as the man's followers troop in behind him. Bejewelled women accompanying the men strut in high heeled boots, wearing tight leather jeans and short jackets to match. These are the girl friends, Greg will learn, as distinct from the wives at home taking care of house, home and children. But Greg isn't into judging.

'Come in…come in…beer all round?' He nods to Steen who jumps to it, delivering jugs of beer to the patrons, finding extra places and offering sandwiches and his mum's piping hot sausage rolls.

Jillian gives her son a reassuring smile. 'Good that I had some ready and waiting in the freezer, aye!' She sees the unspoken question in his eyes. *What's dad got us into this time?*

'Can I get you a drink?' Greg asks Blackbutt.

'A Johnny Walker…that's me drink, but I want to show you somethin' first. Private like.'

'Sure.' Greg leads him to a small table with plenty of leg room beneath it. A private space surrounded by a curved planter where he can see the comings and goings of customers. Blackbutt's hot breath touches his face as he leans in and then, with a quick upward thrust, there it is…an open canvas bag. It has a well-used work-a-day feel to it.

Greg's eyes widen and his throat constricts as he tries to appear calm at the sight of so much cash — bundles of one hundred, and fifty-dollar notes mixed up with tens and fives.

'That…must…add up to…a lot.'

'Haven't countered it yet, but I trust you with it.'

'You don't know me…and what do you mean…trust me with it?'

Blackbutt laughs. 'I know you. I'm a good judge of a man or a woman. And I do my research. I know you've been in business before. Never made a fortune. Too honest for your own good. If I ask you to take care of this while the boys and I have a drink you won't touch it.'

Silence for a moment and then, 'You got a safe, haven't you?'

'Of course, I have a safe and I can put the money away for you while you're here. But tell me, what do I get out of the risk…I mean…?' Bikie gangs, crime, cops…robberies…unexplained deaths. Warning bells clang in Greg's head.

'What…what do I get for my trouble?' Greg squares his shoulders.

'You'll have our trade. And it'll be legit. We have a property not far from here where we meet for our shindigs every month. We drink a lot of beer. Wine, spirits, you name it.'

Blackbutt sits, still and silent while Greg steps away for a moment of quiet. The place is buzzing with voices. Sometimes laughter. It is noisy but no noisier than the footy crowd or the locals on a Thursday after shopping at the supermarkets now springing up in the city's fringes. He goes back to Blackbutt, now standing to face him.

'I would expect your guys to behave as they are now.'

'I'll make sure of it,' says Blackbutt.

'While under my roof, you respect my staff and my place. You live by my rules.'

'Done deal,' says Blackbutt.

So it is that the struggling Wayside pub becomes a lucrative business. Greg loves every minute of it. He hires more staff and that leaves him more time to pursue his sporting interests. That includes organizing teams and raising funds. More often than not he is absent on weekends, while Jillian and Steen manage the business.

'This is so Dad,' Steen remarks one Sunday morning, when yet again, Jillian and he prepare for the Sunday session. 'He and Blackbutt are actually peas in a pod,' he goes on, with a twisted half-smile on his fine boned, sensitive face.

'Oh Steen,' she begins. Jillian knows their son and his girlfriend dream of a working holiday. Steen needs to get on with his own life. *He stays for us and it isn't right.*

'Now, don't start defending him, Mum,' he says. 'What about what you want? Your half-built dream house, for one.'

Instead of the anticipated easy retirement, Jillian works seven days a week but there are lighter moments.

She has mastered the internet, and for the first time in her life has access to Greg's and her joint account. The Jay's orders have tripled their profits. Her plea for extra staff has paid off and given her an occasional afternoon off. Using her own savings, she has organised the builders to resume work on their home in a suburb by the sea. How she loves just to sit by the water, taking in the occasional 'plink' of a leaping fish, or guttural croak of a tern. The soft thrum of gentle waves. One Sunday in a rare moment of intimacy, she had persuaded Greg to accompany her but sensed his reluctance and was disappointed on their arrival.

'Well, have you seen it?' he asked impatiently, 'I have a sport's meeting tonight…and I need to tell Steen how to sort out the bar staff roster. Is the food sorted?'

A turning point comes on what begins as a quiet Sunday afternoon. Greg is away for the entire weekend at a State-wide netball competition in Perth. Jillian and Steen are in charge of the Wayside as usual. She is in the garden when she hears that sound, and for some reason remembers those two peculiar crows, the female floating on her back. Those un-crow like utterings and then the roar…roar of a motorcycle gang. Not the friendly Jay's this time. She knows they are away, on a trip up north. This lot of bikies might not be so respectful. A stab of fear makes her heart race.

Everything is ready. The bar polished to a gleam, glasses and small protectors with the Wayside logo in place. A fine display of wines, red and white and beers on tap. To sooth herself she chooses to play the gentle strains of *Afternoon Delight* on the duke box with wistful memories of distant courtship days.

I can do this, she thinks. *I must. I owe it to Steen to stay strong.* They come in a wave, roaring into the parking lot, some doing tricks by standing on one wheel while revving their engines before swaggering into the Wayside. The few locals present soon leave through the back entrance.

'Drinks'!'' Impatient demands keep Steen on the hop, while Jillian frantically provides sandwiches. This lot are ravenous. In between one job and the next, Jillian makes a hasty call to staff member, Maureen, who needs to drop her children off to her mother's place before arriving to help out.

A central figure in the crowd, headman Thicket, reigns supreme. The bikie's combined breaths and body odours reek of a stale beer smell. A sickly yeastiness, Jillian associates with hard-drinking dart club members who had come by on one of their weekends away from home. They were hungover, but respectful…even apologetic for their dishevelled appearance.

This lot are not. They swagger in, calling for drinks. As he enters the Wayside, Thicket pushes his partner roughly before him, muttering insults. The woman he calls Mash, might have been beautiful in another life, but not this one. Her skin is blotchy, eyes puffed with tears and hair that might have been trimmed recently, now looks bedraggled with straightened ends ratty. It is her hair cut that seems to be a bone of dissention.

'Smarmy dick,' Steen mutters, as they pass.

'Steen, don't talk like that,' Jillian whispers.

'Oh Mum, you're so much the raised in the fifties and sixties nice girl, kind of woman. Even when you say anything in the least bit critical you preface it with: *I don't mean to be awful, or I'm just saying.*'

With a fond smile, Jillian playfully whacks him across the back. 'I'll make more sandwiches. You look after the booze…Ah hello Maureen, thank goodness, you're here.'

Slowly the voices rise, the laughter and comments become louder with ugly insults flying between groups. Thicket holds forth at his table with Mash sitting opposite, her face now tear-stained while he picks at her without mercy. Mash might have been Jillian's own daughter. A good face, now contorted with frustration, despair and rage.

'That was my money, you prick,' says she. 'Money my dad gave me! Gave it to me!'

'You shame me, in front of my mates…I won't have it…how dare you! How dare you spend money on your flamin' hair of all things. Doesn't make you look better if that's what you think. And what about you hitching up with that bastard while I was doin' time?'

'Don't start on that again. Who did you go home to, aye? Your wife!'

'Course I did. But that didn't mean you could stuff around with a bloody Jay of all people. Things get around. People talk, you little bitch.' Enraged, he stands up, his face almost purple, eyes wild. He grabs a chair and facing the window raises it above his head. Alarmed, Jillian moves towards the pair until she is a meter away and that chair is on the point of flying through the window. Already, Jillian sees the outcome in her mind's eye. Glass smashing, great jagged pieces flying into faces. Blood. Mayhem.

Jillian. Softly spoken Jillian. When alone, she will sing in a surprisingly soft but strong contralto. A voice seldom heard under the sweet politeness of her manner. It comes clearly now, full bodied and resonant. A pure voice of protest with almost forty years of unspoken feeling behind it. It comes into the mesmerised silence like the tolling of a warning bell.

'Put that chair down and sit on it,' she cries. 'The police are on their way.'

'The cops?'

'Yes, Sir, the cops!'

*The cops…the cops…the cops…*Every bikie in the Wayside is scrambling to his feet in a bid to be out of there. Even the thickly carpeted floorboards underfoot, judder and shake as if in fear. The roar of the bikie's machines soon fill the air as they roar out of town along a gravel road, leaving a cloud of dust in the air. In the forest nearby the fluttering of many wings fall away as one by one, birds dart home to their rookeries and nests.

'Are the cops really on their way, Mum…and was that really you?'

'No, the cops are not on their way, and yes, there was no time for anything but being me, son,' Jillian` says. 'I wanted those mongrels gone…and I did it. Now you can pour me a drink.'

'But Mum, you don't drink,' says a grinning Steen.

'I'll have a glass of the best Champaign we have…to celebrate my decision.'

'Have you run it past dad?' Steen says with tongue fat in his cheek to make a point.

'No, but I'll tell him as I now tell you,' Jillian says, 'Our house near the sea is finished and I am moving into it. Dad can stay on here if he wants. But not me.'

'Or me,' says Steen, with a grin. 'Don't worry about Dad, he'll do what he wants to do and if it's not us, it'll be somebody else doing his bidding.'

The night is not quite dark yet, but the birds in the nearby bush are asleep with heads under wings with the exception of Mr and Mrs Crow. One, then the other pecks at the grass as though finding treasure, and then, catch the breeze for a little bit of air surfing. As she looks on, Jillian can almost feel it…the flying sensation with wings lifting.

22 Jonesy

Like fugitives, the passengers emerged from the bus shelter. Four figures, wrapped in puffer jackets, eyes squinting against the white glare of headlights. *If I simply drove off without them,* Jonesy reflected, *they won't die of cold.* Light, warm and cheap, the puffer jacket is a winner. Especially among the homeless.

That Jonesy should see himself in that light is unthinkable. What about his present address in town? The cosy and convenient apartment in Perth from way back? The big family home at the tree nursery with its wide acreage on the outskirts of the town? It is the tree nursery in its present state that comes to mind. His skin prickles to go there. A place of empty rooms, with paint flakes falling from ceiling and walls like snow. Roslyn and he had applied it with hope in their hearts…back then.

'I shall paint the corners Mr Arborist,' she told him. Never a drop did she spill. He was smitten by the splendour of her from the moment they met. At another wise dull party, there she was – visiting a mutual friend. The moment they locked eyes, he knew and he was sure she felt the same. Halfway through a law degree – not really her passion – she was happy for a way out. So too the odd modelling job for David Jones. A possible career easy to pass up.

Taking a gamble, Jonesy sold some of the family farm he inherited to set up the tree and plant nursery.

'Pity about that salt effected flat,' he said to Roslyn when, before their wedding day, he introduced her to his patch of the terrain.

'Restore it,' Roslyn said. She had already researched the possibility from the photos he'd shown her. This, after transforming his messy bachelor pad in the city to a welcoming retreat with gourmet meals to top it up.

'What a fabulous cook, you have there, Jonesy.' His friends loved her.

'That's my girl.' He couldn't stop smiling. With Roslyn beside him, he was able to push aside past hurts – the early deaths of his parents and the loss of his first love. But didn't others recover from the loss of parents and move on from the intense experience of first love? The surprise and wonder of it.

As teenagers Katrina and he were drawn to each other like water to water. Their bonding complete when they signed up for ball room dancing. From that first clumsy waltz and mumbled apologies, to mastery. The small town's prince and princess pivoting over jarrah boards made slippery with shaved candle wax.

Their budding relationship fell away the year after Jonesy left for 'Ag' school and Katrina for Melbourne. She came back qualified in physiotherapy. Married and pregnant. Her partner, Stan, a decent bloke, they said. When Jonesy saw her in the street, he knew enough to know a regretful smile when he saw one. *I'm with Roslyn now*, he told her with his eyes.

'I'm opening a clinic. My own,' Katrina said, with the faint gleam of battle in her eyes, while a sweet-faced baby girl peeped at him from her back sling.

'What? You're moving back here, Kat?'

'Yep. Plenty of customers where shearers reside.'

He laughed but bristled at her tone. 'See you, Katrina.' *I won't see you…oh no…*He drew comfort from thoughts of Roslyn, loving the simple practicality of his choice. She would be his helpmate as Katrina never would. Compliant in one way, but fiercely dedicated to him and their joint dream of a stable family and flourishing business.

Safe in Roslyn's arms he murmured, 'We need two boys for the land and two girls for home. Let's get on with it.'

'Really Mr chauvinist,' she laughed. 'Why not two girls for the land?'

'You've been listening to that awful woman on TV, what's her name again? Not half bad looking with her long hair and stunning blue eyes. We blokes aren't interested in what she says, it's her looks that keep us watching…hey stop whacking me with that pillow…'

Back to the present and this cold dark night. Damn it, he hadn't planned on company. It was just him and this ratty old bus for the school and town run. Bought it for a song. *Him and his memories. Why did they cut so deep?* He had it all planned. The end would be quick. He saw the rise…that solid granite cliff, a talisman, a tag mark. Faint from a distance but its cruel outline remained clear. Like an accusing exclamation mark.

'You're less insular and fairer in outlook than many in this town,' somebody told him one boozy night, not long past. Who was it? The new teacher in town? That voice niggled like an itch just when he needed to let everything go. The cliff would be an easy way…a logical way to end it.

It was from that lofty cliff face that he had watched the destruction of an iconic Aboriginal site that surpassed the British Stonehenge in age and national significance, he believed. That image could never be erased in his mind's eye but the site itself was wiped out so easily with a team of front-end loaders. How ironic that he first saw it from the cruel cliff face that now beckoned.

The sky was so clear on that day so long ago. Intensely blue above the spread of dun-coloured farmlands where the ancient site once stood. A small hill, too perfectly circular to be other than something made or modified by human hands. With a circumference of perhaps a half mile. Concentric rings, of waist high stones had been crafted to a uniform size. Each one dented from the pounding of stone on stone. A stone age factory. A highly organised place for making tools and weapons for perhaps a hundred toolmakers.

Jonesy recalled seeing it – as a boy of thirteen walking through the lose layers of stone chips. Such a strange experience and then the shock of a voice. 'Jonesy!' It was a Noongar boy – a boy Jonesy knew from school. 'This is alright…ay?' He suddenly appeared as if from nowhere.

'Todd?' At that time, Todd lived on the native reserve,

one of the smartest boys in school.

'Why don't people know about this site?' Jonesy asked. 'It looks like a kind of factory for lots of people to work at the same time.'

'Them old fellows on the reserve know about it.'

'Shouldn't this place be open for everyone to see?'

'My mob…reckons if people know about it, they'll destroy it.'

'But it looks like that's already happening,' Jonesy said.

Looking back on that day, Jonesy remembered the sound of farm vehicles, and men's voices.

A man from the council called out. 'Young Jonesy out of the way…get home now or you're in trouble…and you…Todd? Back on the reserve where you belong.'

He and Todd had run off and then climbed to the top of the cliff to watch. Ordinary 'decent' blokes in action. Yes, decent, yet blind to the truth of what they were really doing. Farmers who remembered harsh times well. Afraid to lose what they had. They had banded together with bulldozers to reduce the ancient site into a pile of rubble before any busy-body official could stop them. Were they afraid to find another way?

Even as thirteen, Jonesy had wondered. *Shouldn't I tell somebody? Shouldn't this be stopped?*

Jonesy sunk back into his own thoughts and the present, revved the idling engine of the bus and lurched over the gravelled road edge onto the narrow-bituminised way. A broken man. Not a cent left of his fortune. Nothing for his kids. But more than that. He'd been so taken up with other matters, other people and important things, the conscious need for existence had fallen from his grasp.

The words of Isobel, his beloved daughter rang through his head. 'What's so different, Dad? You weren't there for Mum or for me. Lennie feels the same. Stay out of our lives…go back to your trollop.'

Enraged, he had yelled. 'Katrina is a good person. Ask all the people she helps in this damn town. Don't dare speak like that about her…and don't speak for Lennie.' His blood ran hot with helpless anger. Anger with himself and the blasted world. Katrina was a good person, but their latter-day union was as destructive to her as it was to him. Too much guilt lay between them.

He remembered the birth of his first born, a son. That reddish blonde hair…just like his own. *Smart as paint* his maternal grandad always said. Jonesy knew it was true. And it hurt all the more, each time the little boy fought so hard against the only option he and Roslyn could find for his education and future.

'The cottage mum and the teacher at the deaf school is good.' Roslyn and he signed with hands spread. They tried to win him over with smiles, thumbs up and reassuring hugs.

'No, no, no!' Being totally deaf, he croaked his rough version of a few words. Somehow through facial expression and gesture he let them know. *Snuggling in his own cosy bed at night is good. The way his own Mum tucks him into his bed at night is good. The porridge she makes for him is good. Smooth with a hint of honey and a blob of fresh cream on top.*

A pine tree he climbs to the tippy top is good.

'Sorry, I'm on a tight schedule for the Perth run,' the driver of the WA state-run bus service would say. 'I can't wait here all day while you try to fetch him down from the tree, again.'

That bus driver did wait. Time and time again. A decent man, he watched Lennie scuttle down from the pine tree and run for his life, with Jonesy chasing after him. Time and time again, Jonesy held back his own tears, his heart breaking, as he captured and thrust the distraught little boy into Roslyn's arms. Unfailingly, she held him close. Gradually, he would relax, falling asleep in her arms with the drone of the bus and murmur of voices, broken now and then by the driver with the names of towns along the way remembered by Lennie in no particular order…*Mandurah…Mandjoogoordap…Pinjarra…country of tears and regret and then at last, Perth.*

Reconciliation wasn't possible for Roslyn and Jonesy. Not now. Her words rang in his head. 'Where were you, when I needed you? Nothing to say? You were fucking your girlfriend, that's what!'

'Where were you?' he choked back his rage…not at Roslyn, but at fate. It shouldn't have ended like this. Roslyn, away for weeks at a time. Two full term pregnancies. Two still births.

'Yes, where were you, Dad?' Isobel cried. A quiet achiever who worked under the radar. 'It was Mum who made me believe in myself.'

In a cruel twist of fate, over the years, all the love, all the loyalty and sense of homecoming felt by Lennie for his family and home turned to this other world. His deaf companions and the school where Roslyn made strong connections. Volunteered her services, though it meant so much time away from home. This along with those two still births and Isobel's earlier health struggles. How much can a single family suffer?

It seemed that before he could blink, the bachelor apartment in Perth became the centre of family life. The plant nursery, a holiday destination. *Oh, Roslyn what happened to all our dreams?* And yes, he had stepped over the line. It was during Roslyn's many absences at a party with mutual friends that Katrina and he came together. Two lonely people offering the comfort of arms.

'I've waited so long for you,' she whispered. 'I want to be there for you.' From that moment everyone else in his life was seen from a distance, like a landscape on a long drive, wobbling and wavering. An insubstantial mirage-like shimmer.

Nobody was more surprised than Jonesy when confronted by Roslyn. With her departure from his life, after splitting assets, Jonesy' s business plummeted, as did the rejection he saw in people's eyes as they turned away from him. This was a small town with conscious and unconscious biases that ran deep.

'You're like one of us, now bro.' It was his last passenger who spoke. 'Remember that day? I saw you on the cliff top. I saw your face when the bulldozers came, and I knew you felt it too. The loss. The waste of it. We were only kids then. You in the white camp, me in the black.'

'We both knew it was wrong. Oh yes, those

remarkable stones. Our country's history broken.'

Jonesy looked into the man's rugged face. It showed the wear and tear of passing years, but with the same keen, intelligent eyes that he knew.

'Todd, you were a damn smart kid at school. You should have taken up that scholarship and come to university with me.'

'Yeah but no one showed me how to go any further than the third year of highs school. So, I stuck around with my mob and low paid work. Felt safer that way. Happy and sad times spread across time. Remember? You gave me a job once. You gave a lot of people paid jobs and you were a bloody good boss. A fair boss.'

'Thank you, Todd. Glad we spoke tonight. Goodbye.'

'Goodbye, what do you mean?' A see ya tomorrow kind of goodbye?'

'Yeah…yeah…at the bus stop, sharp at eight, see ya.'

Jonesy waited until Todd was out of sight and then turned towards the mountain range. Left instead of right as he intended. Away from the town. Nobody around to notice. Only a few miles more and then to the mountain. After parking the bus and wheezing his way towards higher ground, his eyes on the cliff top, Katrina's words spun in his head. *We need to talk…no, not about us. About you.'*

Several times he stumbled before sitting on a boulder to catch his breath. His hold on the world wavered, slippery and uncertain. He pulled the collar of his puffer jacket closer before climbing the peak to stare at the scene below.

A limpid moon dimmed by mist showed him the flattened landscape with its tell-tale heap of stones that marked the ancient site. Trees had grown-up between boulders lending it an enduring sense of life going on. Some people had that, Jonesy thought. Like Todd Williams who went on making some kind of life, no matter what happened, loyal to his people always.

Looking back to the valley below, Jonesy spotted the flickering lights of a moving car pointing upwards above treetops to the sky and then dipping low to the earth where native shrubs cast shadows. If local, whoever came this way would see the school bus and wonder – perhaps worry that he might be in trouble. People are decent in their own way, he thought. Enlightened one moment, blind as bats in the next.

'No time to waste,' he told himself. *Do the thing you mean to do.*

Jonesy sensed, the earth turning away from the sun while the same old moon cast its light on patches of remnant bushland. And that soil…the indifferent cloying soil that hid the bones of its people, black and newbie white fellas, layers of history fifty million years long. Among the dead, Jonesy's children who never got to breathe sweet air. He mourned for them now, breaking a drought of tears that had gone on…too long. He mourned…for his lost self and for the marriage with Roslyn that began with such hope. He wept a flood of tears until the sound of his mutterings became shaky and weird.

Too exhausted to do anything but breathe, he took in the sound of voices. His son's voice that was equally weird but not shaky. Lennie, his courageous boy calling in the croaky voice he used when unable to sign. His boy, who embraced life with joyful vigour, always. When he came, Lennie's arms were a vice.

'Dad?' That was Isobel, his daughter. 'Oh Dad…you wouldn't…' She went on, holding back tears. 'Mum and Darren are on a tour but we've been in touch. She said to thank Todd and Katrina for letting us know they were worried about you.'

Jonesy looked past his daughter and son to Todd, his rugged face visible in the light from Katrina's torch. Held in the arms of all four, he could only sob. 'I'm sorry…I'm sorry…'

23 Love Sickness

1930

Milani, that girl of Ricardo's – she needs a husband and now it looks like it will happen. Her father re-reads the letter from his friend, Antonio who has established Romagna, a farm in Western Australia. He's doing well too.

Tight! Antonio is as tight as his old man. But his son, Niccolo needs a wife as it happens. Niccolo is a good worker, primed to take over Emilia, a second family farm a few miles from a township in the southwest.

Blood rushes to Milani's face when she hears her parents discussing the matter. The usually neat slipstitch that graces the hem of a special nightdress for her trousseau wavers off line. So, it is really happening…marriage. The dream of every Italian girl, isn't it? Encouraged by gossiping relations and friends, Milani is the archetypal sister in waiting. Blushing furiously, she escapes to her room upstairs to examine his photograph without onlookers minding her business. A small image taken with a little box camera; he looks to be tall with soulful dark eyes. She crosses herself to say a heartfelt thank you to the Holy Mary and Jesus, because he is beautiful. Not that good looks are everything. But she can't help drooling over him. She kisses the photograph then holds it close to her heart uttering a crooning sound not so very different from the brood pigeon fluttering outside the shuttered window.

In a half dream state, she feels it. A mix of pleased excitement, fear and nostalgia. Never again will she be single and in this small room with the echo of footsteps on marble floors, the calls of her people floating above ancient walls with the ornate signature of craftsmen and artists long gone. Away from her language and culture. She peers at his photograph again. This stranger who has been chosen for her.

They say he will *get on*, whatever that means. It doesn't matter. 'I will love him. I will love him with all my heart,' she whispers.

'She's a virgin,' his father tells Niccolo. 'And you'll treat her right.' The words remind West Australian born Niccolo, of church, of sin and all the things he is not allowed to do. He learned it all at 'Bushy Week' from nuns with some of the 'boy stuff' from the good Father himself. They instruct kids from the farms about being good Catholics. You must not have impure thoughts that can make you have a wet dream in the middle of the night or coax your willie into a life of its own. But he's a grown man and what he does in the middle of the night is his own damn business.

Milani arrives in Australia before he is ready for it. Arrives with her broken English, he barely understands. With hair pulled back from her face, her Romanic features stand out, unadorned somehow. Raw. Like a newborn when old aunties will claim a likeness to some long lost relative. Her deep brown eyes are wide with apprehension.

He doesn't want this girl and she knows it, within seconds. When their eyes meet, her face suffuses with colour. Her full Roman lips tremble.

Oh, for God's sake she's going to cry.

Alone in the room that Angelina, Niccolo's mother, has prepared for her, Milani finds a pretty embroidered pillow cover and matching quilt. In a state of disbelief, she sits on the stool before the dressing table mirror, turning away from the reflection of her own stricken face. She holds back a great dam of tears, her whole being heavy with sorrow and homesickness for her own *madre* and *sorella*. She hears but doesn't quite understand Niccolo hissed whisper. 'She looks…she looks so…like…a *ding*. Are you sure she's not a cousin?'

Angelina turns on her son furiously, breaking into the lingo, as he calls it, then crosses herself, praying to the Holy Mary and Joseph for divine intervention. Prays for poor Milani, hoping Niccolo will change his mind, yet knowing, with a mother's heavy heart, her son will never accept this girl.

He is not acting like a true Italian son. While he eats everything, she cooks for him with gusto, he hankers after the kind of food his Australian friends eat. 'Why can't we have a roast of lamb cooked in dripping like other people have? And now you want to suffocate me by marrying me off to somebody I don't know.'

From outside the guest room, Milani hears but doesn't

quite understand every word. She recognises the distant sound of cackling hens and the fierce barking of farm dogs she'd rather not know. This is the family's *new house,* Angelina's pride and joy with a guest room that feels hollow. Unlived in, and silent, yet full of echoes. Where are all the people? With the metallic smell of new paint in her nostrils she longs for the sounds and smells of her tiny room at home surrounded by people who care about her. At home with busy streets that hum with people going about their business. She wants to be home with her dreams intact.

'Oh, my *Madre…*and *Sorella…*' Will she ever see them again?

Niccolo storms out of the house, taking off on his Indian motorcycle, proudly sold to him just last week by a pioneer of the brand. Almost a coming-of-age gift from his father, but really in lieu of unpaid wages. He revs the engine, slipping for a moment on the build-up of gravel as he turns onto the newly graded road, then surges onwards through the township to the other family farm, Emilia. *My farm,* he thinks. At a lesser speed, he turns into the southern entrance – over the cattle pit before coming to a stop.

Sitting astride the motorbike, Niccolo takes in the scene. One day he will build his dream house on the rise opposite - above the swiftly flowing stream that cuts his farm in two. He'll use trees from his uncleared land for building a house. Beautiful jarrah made into boards at the privately-owned timber mill nearby. There'll be a veranda all round his house and he will plant pencil pines, one on each side of the stone steps at the front…they will lead to a rose garden.

On this day his eyes focus on the creek, at the point where it disappears among the bulrushes, recalling the last time he saw her – Estelle, wife of their farmworker, Freddie Bennet. On a hot day, she will paddle in bare feet along the water's edge, with her small daughter by her side. The bright pink of her skirt standing out against the green reeds as she moves with a dreamy kind of rhythm, like a waterbird, he thinks. Where is she today? Why is it, he 'places' her every time he comes to work on this new place his father called *Emilia*.

On the other side of town, Niccolo's mother, Angelina does her homework. She visits a widower, Luigi who needs a wife. The nuggetty man lifts his battered felt hat and nods his approval when he sees Milani's photograph. With a potato crop almost ready to dig, an extra pair of hands will be welcome, he tells her. He's too busy to visit right now, but will Angelina and Ricardo arrange the wedding with the good Father please?

'I can't…I can't.' Milani can't bring herself to argue with Angelina but her daughter, Grace gives her shoulder a friendly squeeze.

'You don't have to marry Luigi if you don't want to…' She speaks more urgently but slowly in a mix of English and Italian.

Milani understands. Grace is Niccolo's sister…his 'sorella'. She's married to a big fair haired Australian, an

'Aus-sie!' His name is Ben and she sees that he is the only one who can make his father-in law, laugh. Grace and Ben live in the township now and have their own carting business.

'Oh yes, my parents are happy with us now but it wasn't always like this. We had to run away together."

'How…you do that?' Milani's deep sad eyes widen in awe of this girl who wears bright red lipstick.

'Ben borrowed his dad's old Chev. A runabout with room for my brother and his sister on the back. They witnessed our marriage at the Bridgetown Registry Office and then we celebrated with a drink at Scott's Hotel.'

She says it again. 'If you really don't want to, then don't marry Luige…he's too old and set in his ways…a grumpy old coot, wanting more money for his wizened potatoes than they're worth.'

A grumpy old coot, that sounded awful. Milani's troubled face looks on the point of tears. 'How…how I find money to live? Where I live?'

'You can live with Ben and me while you look for a job…work…like…sewing. I've seen your needlework, it is…beautiful. Our friend Alec is a tailor and he's opened a shop. He can't keep up with the demand for men and women's tailored coats and suits. He's desperate to employ somebody like you.' She goes on. 'Alec is from a Macedonian migrant family whose dad came from a long line of tailors in the old country. Ben and I love them to bits…Alec is handsome…and single,' she adds with a mischievous grin. 'If you can't use a sewing machine, he'll teach you in a jiffy.

'What this jiffy?'

'Oh Milani…oh you're coming home with Ben and me and I'll dress you for an interview for your first job in Australia.' Grace smiles to herself. Her mind racing…let loose that dark hair with its golden lights. A touch of rouge on those pale cheeks…

At Emilia, Freddie, the farm worker has the draft horses in harness and is ploughing in the far paddock. A wizard with horses, Freddie can break a bush brumby or work a team, snig logs, plough a field. Doesn't mind mucking out a pigsty or rising in the middle of the night to stoke a clearing fire. Patient. A patient man. That's why Niccolo and his father hired him. Came in a horse and cart loaded with household goods. Willing to accept a low wage in exchange for the house. The deserted soldier settler's place for his woman, Estelle, and their small daughter, Jodie.

While Niccolo checks on the herd of young heifers mooching in the paspalum for sweet green shoots along the creek line, he finds himself looking towards the worker's cottage to see if he might see her – Estelle, and the child who might be collecting kindling to light the kitchen stove each morning or checking for deliveries in the mailbox near the gate.

'What's the name of Freddie's Mrs now?' he will ask whenever she is mentioned, though he knows her name and almost everything about her. A slender waist. The way she smooths the apron around her middle. The outline of her breasts under the faded house dress. She seems taller than her actual height though he reckons she'd be level with his shoulder.

Right now, after escaping his mother's angry gaze he takes in the progress of what will be his farm. Four young chestnut saplings he planted beside the creek are beginning to look like trees with large green leaves ruffled by the wind – green…silver…green. Niccolo and his dad have plans to partially block the creek, with two giant red gums already felled. He can see it in his mind's eye. A lake, to be seen from a future house on the hill above.

'My place,' Niccolo whispers. The disquiet of family tension dissipates. His parent's displeasure…the sad Italian girl recedes from his mind and conscience. *I cannot…I will not.* His whole being relaxes. *I am here now.*

When Niccolo first saw Estelle beside Freddie on a horse drawn cart, he recognised something precious in her, yet immovable too. She would never agree to marry a stranger…or be beholden to anyone.

One day she'll be mine.

Where did that thought come from? Without Freddie's help he'd never get to where he wanted to be…away from his father's heavy hand.

One wild winter morning, after rain and hail, Freddie arrives at the cow shed to do the milking, looking worried. Wash from the downpour has flooded between and above the jarrah slabs that have been laid in lieu of a proper veranda at the entrance to his house.

'Finish the milking Freddie and don't worry,' says

Niccolo with a measured air. Though his heartbeat quickens, he takes his time. He is a little afraid of Estelle. In quieter moments she looks like the Saint Theresa of his mum's holy pictures, but not always. Not at all.

One day he had been sharpening a cross-cut saw blade in the shed near the worker's cottage when he saw her fighting with the wind in an attempt to hang out a line of household linen to dry. As soon as the wind cupped the double sheets, the forked prop holding the clothesline up, shuddered with the weight of its load and then collapsed like a fallen soldier.

'Damn and blast,' she let out a scream of frustration and then, looking up at the indifferent sky, muttered. 'The sky doesn't give a damn and nor does anyone.'

Niccolo had been with his father when she made a complaint. 'You didn't think it out when you made the damn thing, or think it was important enough to take the trouble.' Beyond the worker's house paddock, the ring-barked trees stood forlornly, their bare limbs stretched against the stormy sky. Only the shed out the back stood firm. On that day it seemed to Niccolo more trustworthy than the unlined house with gaps between roughly hewn jarrah boards that let in an icy drift of air on cold winter nights.

Niccolo had slept there on occasions before Freddie and Estelle moved in and knows just how cold it can be.

Now, she struggles with runoff from the downpour swamping the sleepers that do for a veranda, brushing her doorstep. Using a shovel that is too big for her, Estelle attempts to divert the runoff.

'Shall I?' Niccolo's father who had arrived by truck, gives a curt nod while Estelle stands back.

Flexing his muscles, unconsciously enjoying the roll of rescuer, Niccolo takes up his own spade to dig a trench for drainage and quietly fashions a bridge with boards.

'It is strong enough to take a wheelbarrow of wood across,' he tells her, though she appears not to hear him, as she focusses on his father.

'I need something more permanent for drainage and a proper clothesline…what is it with you men? You build a shed or even a house with care, but you're hopeless when it comes to clotheslines. I've never met a man yet, who put up a decent one…you're always too busy to see to the things that really matter.'

'Your husband must see to these things. It's not my business.' Antonio turns on his heel and strides away. Away from her angry retort.

'You keep my poor Freddie working from early morning to late at night…and he's not a well man. There's no time for him to look after the house you own…that's right walk away from what you don't want to hear!'

'Ah…stupid woman!' Antonio mutters. '

Later he tells Niccolo, 'She's sure to kick up a fuss when she's told that you'll be boarding there until we build a decent shed for you.

'What?' He holds his tongue – with a mix of anger and apprehension. The plan has been to build a solid shed on stumps with an attic and a jarrah floor that will do for him to live in until they can afford to build a proper house.

'You'll pay her board money?' Niccolo can barely look at his father.

'For a bit, and then, you'll pay her. There's too much time wasted travelling between home and here…and I must tell you and tell you straight, you are still responsible for Milani's grief!' His father hasn't given up on the idea of their marriage even if Angelina and the girl herself have. That much is clear to Niccolo.

It is Freddie who tells Estelle the news about their new boarder, guiltily, as if it were his fault. 'It won't be for long, love,' he soothes.

'So, the big useless son will be in the house from now on,' Estelle grumbles. Not really useless, she thinks but it is the only word that comes to mind. There is a room at the back of the cottage that will do for him, a small add-on at the end of a porch.

'Let him freeze.' She does not want this boy-man in her house. He rattles her somehow. A gust of wind whistles and sighs against the windowpane, penetrating gaps in the timber walls. The strange metallic cry from a flock of black and white cockatoos swoop into the grove of pines for the ripening cones. *One for sorrow, two for joy…three for disappointment.* The chant plays in Estelle's head. Superstitious nonsense but she senses a shadow like 'something' hovering. Something to disturb the peace and safety of their first little home. Estelle hates change. Always has.

'What Mummy?' Jodie wraps soft baby arms around her middle.

'I didn't say anything, darling, but come by the fire and

we'll warm ourselves.' Estelle throws banksia nuts and pinecones on the open fire in the lounge room. It is bare except for two cane chairs.

'His highness will need to bring his own damn chair,' she mutters.' With Jodie on her lap, she nuzzles into her daughter's downy head. Jodie sometimes has a hurt look that hurts Estelle equally. They are both safe and warm, now, she thinks. Safe with Freddie to take care of them. She remembers how much she relied on him in those foggy days after Jodie's birth when she struggled to make sense of the world, days flowing into nights made less troubling by Freddie's reassuring voice. 'I have fed baby Jodie and now she sleeps.' His gentle lullaby would flow into her own dreams, softening and then dissolving irrational fears. She sees now, how she learned to be a mother through Freddie. He brought a gentle love to her life she has never experienced before. A broken soldier from the war and her, in desperate need of somebody who cared.

'Read me a story, Mummy?' Jodie turns to her with innocent eyes.

'I'll sing you a song instead. Which one?'

'The moon song, Mummy.'

'Are you sure? We always sing the moon song.'

'Yes, yes. The Moon song. I want the moon song.'

Estelle smiles and sings: *Oh, lady moon*
your horns point towards the east
Shine, shine, be at peace, be at peace…

Niccolo stands at the door, afraid to knock. 'Go to the

house for your morning break,' his father commanded. And here he is, outside her door, mesmerised by her voice. Surprisingly sweet but strong…the voice of a woman brave. Brave enough to stand up to his father who is unbending as a rod of steel.

'Estelle,' he says her name and it pleases him. He wants her to see him. She nettles him. Captures him. He wants to be with her. Just twenty-four and he is in love.

While Niccolo will sleep peacefully in the bed Estelle unwillingly makes for him, on his father's farm, Milani takes in the muted sound of Ricardo snoring from across the passage. A curlew calls. To this Italian girl, a strange foreign cry in the night and then a more familiar pigeon calls for a mate. A mournful coo…coo…coo, on and on, with no answering call. Carefully and swiftly Milani rises from her bed, takes up the special hand-sewn nightdress she has already laid out. With the garment held close, she rips it to shreds. Then takes scissors from her sewing kit to cut Niccolo's photograph into tiny pieces. Bundling all together in her empty sewing basket, she leaves the darkened house and heads for the smouldering incinerator in the back yard. Stuffs the basket's contents into its sluggish embers and then stands to watch the flames take hold, flare into life and then die in a nest of hot coals.

Taking in the bitter smell and taste of burnt cloth, she moves away, breathing clean cold air in great gulps. With her back to the house, she looks at the silhouettes of trees against the sky. After a frightening storm it is clear now and the stars have a washed look and the moon – the dear old moon is still there. Milani recalls all that Grace said.

There is so much to take in. So much to learn. Though still shaken she knows she will recover, but always mourn a little for the loss of something precious…something she never really had…her very first love.

24 Forbidden Stories

My dear Lily, I want to tell you there were reasons I drove away without speaking to you. We are sisters. I should have been there to see it all through. It was just that I couldn't bare another moment of being in that house with smoke drifting in from Noah's bonfire in the back-yard. The stink of smoke felt to me like a dreadful metaphor for the way we lived.

It infiltrated into the cloth of Mama's lace curtains imported all the way from Italy, as she would tell us in that 'plum in the mouth' way she affected. As I drive into the shimmering landscape towards the city and my new life, I have a sense of home coming. For Dadda will be there and hopefully, one day, you and Noah too. It's where I found true happiness you know. It's where I discovered a kind of normalcy and openness in family relationships I had never experienced before. It's a place where I don't need to hide anything.

I can't help resenting Noah's doggedness in wanting to 'burn the damn lot of it'. I know how bitter he is for losing an inheritance that was promised to him. One that bound him to the property and to Niccolo's name and will. Our brother was let down badly. And as much as I loved Mama, there is something in me that resents those letters you saved on my behalf.

'Mama wanted you to have them,' you told me. So here they are, just where you put them, on the back seat of my car with my beach towel thrown over them in case Dadda should see. Perhaps he has seen them. Maybe he read every one. Who knows who knew what in our family? We are not great talkers. Even after the breakup, no words were spoken.

For you and me, it didn't matter, in fact it made us even closer. We didn't need to talk. To this day, we still fit together like right and left gloves, even with the difference in our height and size. After Dadda and I moved away, I loved coming back to spend time with you, walking arm in arm down the gravel road between Mama's house and Dadda's with the trees on either side reaching over us. Same mother, different fathers. Our tunnel of green, we called it, and didn't we gasp, sputter and swear at any neighbour who might pass us in their runabouts or trucks, spewing great clouds of dust or in winter, spattering us with orange-brown mud? They knew better than to offer us a lift. You even looked like Mamma at such moments…nobody could turn on a haughty look like she could, or stare down anyone who dared to be cheeky.

Oh, my darling sister, it wasn't all so terrible, was it? There were good times, weren't there? Remember those big sparky fires at night, when the men were clearing the land? We all sat around the fires on blocks of cut wood, roasting potatoes in hot ashes. And the night of the Aurora Australis, when the sky was pink all over with flickering shades of green. Small bats flew way above us, diving for insects and being fooled by small stones thrown up by the men.

Remember? We made daisy chains when our days went on, the minutes and hours, days and weeks, uncounted, with no sense of an ending. Taken and filled with the here and the now of childhood. Blue sky, close and far. Yellow wattle and blue bush. Sun browned hands making daisy chains. There were sad times too, when I climbed the pine tree and I saw Dadda ploughing with the new motorised Ferguson tractor. Round and round…as if he didn't really know or care what he was doing. I heard him cry that night. A broken man crying without tears. I felt his pain as sharp as a badly scraped knee in that second before it bleeds.

We were such innocents, you and I. Then there was Noah, our brother (your brother, my half-brother strictly speaking). Noah, the loner trying so hard to fit in. It wasn't lack of intelligence that earned him Niccolo's fury or at school, the heavy hand of Sister Bee. She belted him most days for being late – never asking why. Never knowing that Niccolo made him milk a dozen cows before heading off to school each day.

All three of us suffered I know, but you and I had each other while Noah, poor innocent, had nobody. He hated school where he spent most of his time longing to be home with his pigeons. Yet he tried so hard to be like other people and would hang around, somehow knowing he wasn't wanted. He tried to tell me in his halting way about sitting on the Walters' back step, sheltering from the drizzle of rain with a super bag folded to make a cape over his head and shoulders. You can picture him, sucking air through his teeth as he did when out of his element. But he was hungry for acceptance. The three Walters children with fair rosy skin and big innocent eyes, stared at him, warily, but curious.

One day he went over there looking for a lost cow, wondering if it had joined the Walters' herd. The house appeared empty but the kitchen door was open. Out of curiosity he peeped inside. Everything shiny and neat with a warm fire in the stove, a vase of pink carnations, bottled fruit in glass bottles and a savoury smell that made his mouth water. Then the shock of it when the children's mother came in from one of the bedrooms. She looked frightened.

'Don't ever come in here without knocking.' She sent him out and then her little boy came running after him holding out a jam sandwich.

'For you, from my mummy,' he said.

When Mama was told about it,' she tossed her head proudly. 'As if we don't feed him!' she snapped.

When I did a portrait of Mama at school, Mr Harrison told me I'd made her look like the Mona Lisa. I giggled foolishly, wanting to ask if the Mona Lisa dropped her aitches too. But there was a kind of softness in Mama – she could charm anybody and I could see the way Mr Harrison looked at her with such curiosity that he wanted to know her. You and I know, Mama was no easy touch.

I was there when she breathed her last breath. There's no way I would desert her even though Niccolo ran away like a scared rabbit. It was Dadda she turned to and Dadda who nursed her – nursed her till the end.

There is nothing like the stillness and silence of death. There's no going back. No words to be heard or to be said. It is over…her body now a tiny thing, fragile as a shell washed up on a shore. Just a moment before, slick and shiny from the life that was in there and then gone.

Our mother had a kind of delicacy…a 'preciousness' never going beyond her capabilities. Not like you and I, who almost always go beyond the call of duty. No, mother was mindful of herself and doing what she did well. She had the kind of beauty that made men love her. Even though I try to put her out of my head, she is with me always. The evenness of her breathing, the smell of her skin and that perfume…She would rub it into her hands and then rub it into mine.

Though I couldn't find the words to explain I knew from the very beginning we were not like other people. And then I grew used to it. Like Mamma's curtains in the lounge room. Brought all the way from Italy from the lace makers of Burano…that was Niccolo's doing of course and God help us if we so much as touched them. He'd tell us how much they cost him.

'Mean bastard,' Noah once said and his face flushed red. I wanted to hug him for speaking the unspeakable.

You become accustomed to things as they are, and it's too frightening to question or change it. Dadda believed and I believe it too. Like the pattern on the linoleum on the kitchen floor. I was never happy unless it shone like glass. Like putting a gloss on those hot summer days and the dullness of long afternoons. The shiny floors were never mother's doing. That was our job, remember?

Rubbing in the polish, I can still smell the waxiness, and then shining each section to a gleam. We put old jumpers on our feet and danced.

Remember?

Mrs Bradford used to cut through our place to visit her brother and his family. She'd pinch some roses from our garden if ever she got the chance. The Sargant children cut through our place too, running past as if they were frightened of us or if it looked like we weren't home they peeped through the fence and stared for ages, then filled their school bags with chestnuts from under the spreading trees near the big slab hut.

'I've been in Niccolo's hut heaps of times,' I once told you. 'When I was small.' Your big brown eyes widened. 'Oh, but we're not allowed,' you whispered. Then of course it became Dadda's when the rest of us moved into the new house on the hill.

Did I love my mother? Of course I did. We all worshipped her…didn't we? Every one of us competed for her attention. I can still see her as she was when we were children. Small and neat. A beautiful woman with tiny hands and feet. Even I felt clumsy and ungainly beside her.

I wonder if those letters are full of trite things, like the weather, and her trip down to the gate to check for mail, bread, and meat delivered to our box. Whether we all had colds…whether she'd cooked a roast and left a meal in the oven for Owen. Once he bought home one of the Sargant boys after they'd been rabbiting and they shared his meal. I could tell Owen was embarrassed. But Tom

Sargant was not…as if he had to show Owen how to cope with a friend in your house. How to greet somebody…when to arrive and when to leave. We did not have friends, or if we did get near to it with somebody at school, it soon fell away.

There's an extravagant impulsiveness in me that wants to tear her unsent letters into shreds and throw them from a cliff into the sea. Call it a kind of suicide or a fitting end to unwanted memories. I was with Mama before you were born, my beautiful sister, remember that. There from the beginning. It was just Dadda, Mama and me. Farm workers. And after Niccolo moved into the hut near the chestnut trees, Mama crawling into my bed in the early hours, warming her frozen feet against mine.

One life is surely enough for Mama. Why should I re-live what has already been lived? I can't imagine our mother revealing anything about the why of it. Why Dadda stayed on for so long after Mama and we kids moved into the new house with Niccolo.

Of course, Niccolo called on Dadda to take care of Mama when she was ill. Though I helped Dadda nurse her when her defences were low, she never did break the ridiculous code of silence that governed our lives. Never spoke about the past. As if she could let it all go by and enter a brand-new day with equanimity. While we, poor injured things tried to make sense of a world not one of us was equipped to deal with.

Now she has left us, here we are, a fractured family, like Humpty Dumpty who fell off the wall. It's a kind of irony that now she is gone, we three will follow Dadda.

He has a place near mine, in a northern suburb of the city where there are still tracts of bushland with orchids in the season. But let us remember the here and now of our childhood. When blue is the sky, close and far. Our hands, sun browned with eager fingers reaching for yellow petalled flowers. Capeweed of all things. Taints the milk but we don't mind. We try to make the longest daisy chain in the world. We fill the days with no sense of an ending.

I remain, your soul mate and loving sister, Jodie.

25 Scars

The summer of 1996 — another hot day cracks wide open. Aiden lies in a sweat, trying to let go his dream. Trying to let go Bosnia. He is here now in gentle Busselton with its quiet back streets, among the pigeons and the peppermints. The soft rustle and swirl of the sea at the end of the street. He squints against the stark light of the window, reminding himself to get a life. Yet knowing he'll go on as he is, with barely enough energy to get himself a meal, never mind a job. As for friends, who'd want to know him?

It's my choice to be alone. That's what he told the psychologist. A young graduate, she'd been a little afraid of him. He'd seen it in her eyes and in the relieved sigh she let out when he refused another appointment. He might have told her about the dream. How he was always the victim in his dream. It was always a Serb who had a boot on his chest. A gun brushing his throat.

He pads into the bathroom and rinses his face. Gazes sourly at his reflection. Ugly black stubble, mud-puddle eyes. Like a battlefield. Taking a razor from the cabinet he scrapes away at his whiskers without bothering to use soap or shaving cream. The black stubble falls into the basin, clogging the outlet. To clean it he turns on the tap at full pressure, disliking himself for not caring about the wastage.

An image comes to him…a haunting memory of war that plagues his dreams. He cannot let it go. Once a teacher and musician, now ex-outlaw soldier caught up in his father's war. A deserter in hiding, when the woman stumbled upon him on the mountain slope. A devout Muslim, she might well have given him away but chose to save his life. Heavily pregnant, she scrambled below to fetch him water, came back from her farm house with food.

Aiden drank a glass of chlorinated scheme water from the tap, remembering the crystal-clear water of a mountain stream. Icy and clean on his throat. From the apartment next door, comes the sound of Luke's trumpet. The kid is good, but he needs help with his breathing technique with the higher notes. If he had the energy, Aiden would tell Jenni and offer to help, but then she would surely give him that queer look that reminds him of just how scary he looks. It is the scar - a bloody great streak that came without warning. It runs like a small river from his right eye socket to his chin. A deep rut. Red-purple. Against his pale skin – quite the work of art.

He goes to buy bread, conscious of the scar glowing like a regular neon sign. By the surly expression of the man in the Save-Way shop, it is proof of his danger to the safety and order of things. That and his dark looks. The man mutters about bloody refugees and Australia being for Australians. *Hey, mate, I went to school here,* Aiden wants to say in his best ocker drawl, but the effort is too much. His face feels hot and the scar itches unmercifully.

It is only when he meets the boy along the street that his discomfort dissipates.

'Hey, Aiden! Mum's not working today.' Luke's eyes light up with happy recognition. 'We're going to chill out on the beach at Meelup. You ought to come.'

If the wind comes in there'll be waves and he plans to test his surfboard while his Mum does her writing. On a scale of one to ten, the day feels lighter. Aiden eats breakfast. Fresh bread with cheese and hot sweet tea. Maybe he will drive to Meelup. People do that kind of thing. They spread themselves on towels between swims, happy just to be there as he once did. But that was before he'd gone back to his father's homeland to fight a no-win ethnic war. His pre-war life is null and void. Finished.

The midday sun beats down. There is a shift in the wind and the waves rush in. Aiden pulls his hat over his eyes. All morning he's been trying to keep his face away from the boy's mother in case she sees the scar at its worst. Some people have the power to make it deeper and nastier than it is. It is difficult because he quite enjoys watching Jenni. Her clear golden skin. The way she smiles at the boy with transparent love, especially when he calls out, 'Mum, did you see that!' And then she will go back to her work with a faint smile on her lips, murmuring words with a rhythm he recognises as poetry. It reminds him of his other life as a musician when he tried to write lyrics. In another life, he might have colluded with her. In another life he was always listening for new sounds, for new arrangements.

Aiden finds himself listening now. To the sound of

the sea, the gentle suck and coil of waves, a shift in pace, a long rolling whoosh. In the scrub between the sea and the street, cicadas chirp out their mating songs and from far away, gulls call. Drowsy with the sun on his limbs, he drifts. Images of the boy, of the woman, of the sea, melt into dreams. Rocks, sand, sea. His scar, running over the sand like a stream.

'I'm thirsty, Mum,' said the boy.

'Then drink from the stream,' said the woman.

Now, there is somebody shaking him.

'Are you okay?'

Jenni kneels beside the man. Behind her, the boy is a tiny figure on his surfboard, a brush stroke against the bright blue water. But her eyes are directly on his face. She stares at him with frank curiosity. At once he puts his hand on his cheek. The scar's intensity shoots right up. He flinches as she reaches out to touch it, but gives way to her calm assertiveness. He is amazed at her accuracy. With gentle fingers she traces its every nuance.

'My God, that must be hurting.' She tut-tuts over him until he feels obliged to explain.

'Trouble is, it ain't your regular kind of scar,' he says, flippantly.

'That's beside the point, its deep. And it's hurting the person you are.' She regards him clinically, as a doctor might, in that pause before the moment of decision, with the whoosh and roll of the sea the only sound between them. He half expects her to write a prescription, but now she reflects quietly on his case. 'I think you'll be okay.' She explains that in her case, writing poetry helps.

'It's dark sometimes,' she adds, 'and probably not that good as far as poetry goes.' Pretty Jenni with her wide smile, her Irish blue eyes and a letter box to match.

'But why?'

She tells her story in a matter-of-fact way. Lays it bare. Luke's father got himself shot in troubled Ireland. She had been dragged along with him in a deadly game of paybacks, until it made her sick. 'I got out. But yes, the memories have to go somewhere or you're dead.'

They are sitting together when the boy runs out of the sea, his skin shining and wet, his words tripping over his tongue. He is stoked and starving. Are they going to buy fish and chips and is Aiden coming too? But a swim first. Jenni looks at him and he nods. No question.

The boy watches with a towel around his shoulders. At first Aiden is with his mother and then he is not.

While Jenni skims the edges, Aiden dives into deep-water. Dives deep. How does Jenni remain so beautiful, so alive? So undamaged? She deserves a place in the sun. In the light, not in his darkness. Down, down deep, and deeper still, he dives into a world of dreams. He sees strange animals or are they people? A Serb in full battle attire, making rude gestures at Aiden for handing him over to his murderous kinsmen. And there is the Muslim woman who saved him. Simply because he was a wounded man. A deserter without food or water. He sees what might have been his rescuer now, floating like a vo-luminous mini whale, enormously pregnant, reproving him for being on the side of rapists.

But now the woman sighs, and hands him a cup, he,

grabbing it with both hands. *Thank you…Oh thank you.* The cup refills itself, its contents spilling over him. Cool, seductive, like a blanket. He is drowning in liquid that comes like milk from the woman. Drowning is a strangely peaceful death, they say, though no one has ever come back to prove it. The Serb, no longer hostile, grins broadly and the woman too, as if they know that in death everything dissolves. All hatreds. He feels like crying. He has come home…This is where he belongs, but there are hands reaching, grabbing any part of him until they take hold.

Insistent hands tug at his hair. It is gentle Jenni being her most ungentle self, dragging him after her. With her first breath of fresh air, she yells at him.

'Stubborn bastard! Scar or not, you're here to stay.'

Together they struggle back to the shallows with fine white sand beneath their feet, the sun, a great golden ball, slipping behind the sea and the boy running to meet them.[2]

---

[2] Previously published in WA Literary Magazine edited by Alwyn Evans of Fremantle Press.

26 Frog Music

I am six years old and I am cold in the green painted bed my Dad made for me. Through the window, there is just enough light for me to get up and make my way across the cold linoleum floor, past my big sister's bed and little sister's cot to the chamber pot. I do a wee and then shuffle through the kitchen, through the lounge to the front veranda where Mum and Dad sleep. Though we call it the front veranda, it faces not the front gate but a back wilderness of swamp and bushland.

'Mummy, I'm cold,' I say, hearing the pleading in my own voice.

'Oh no,' she sighs, lifting the bed clothes with her feet to make a space for me at the bottom of the bed. 'Now go to sleep.'

I snuggle into the warmth and then turn my gaze to the sky, taking in the overarching sound of a frog concert less than two hundred metres away. The swamp is heaven to we children, our playground and refuge.

In time I will learn to swim in its deepened scooped out centre. Following my brothers' lead, a few years on again and I make a canoe all by myself from a sheet of corrugated iron, using one of Dad's hammers to bang the ends together, then seal it with tar from the drums Dad has been given by a gang of road makers. Testing my craft in the swamp I am transported into the story land of Huckleberry Finn on the Mississippi River. But I digress, right now I am at the bottom of Mum and Dad's bed, safe from all enemies.

If the Japanese invade, as the editor of the West warns, I'll be running as fast as I can through soft tipped swamp loving shrubs to our giant banksia tree. I'll be perfectly safe in its bendy arms with a good supply of water from the freshwater spring beneath it. These plans I make within the security and warmth of my parent's bed and the wonder and magic of frog song filling the night.

In time I will learn the orchestra of these little creatures who surely include moaners, hooters, hummers, quackers, tappers and more. But for five-year-old me, the voices blend as one, until old man bullfrog belts out a solo, loud and resonant.

With guidance from our nature loving mother, I will learn and know these creatures and their transformational life cycle from tadpole to frog.

Frogs in a well, frogs in a creek, frog song filling the night.

With sadness I drive past what was once 'our place', wanting to look away from the flattened swampland, now a shallow pool with a single tree left standing. Sometimes in vain now, my ears ache for frog song.

27 That Boy Jacob

It is heading towards summer 1947 when Jacob puzzles over the big questions. Water and oxygen make the earth unique in our known universe. That's what the book says. He carries the book in his swag, along with his best strides, shirt and tie, best shoes and working clothes. The book is one thing he has from his dad. Dad the sailor man. Here today, gone tomorrow. Maybe he'll be a sailor too…maybe…one day. But Jacob doesn't want to be here today and gone tomorrow. He wants to find a place, and to stay.

Through the gap in the iron clad roof of Mr Nowak's shed, the crisp night air wafts over Jacob's face. Better still, it shows him the stars. So alluring and bright out here in the sticks. He thinks he might stay awake all night, just to see that vast universe and how the Southern Cross appears to move as the earth turns over. Out there – in space, a trillion other worlds revolve and here he is in this one. Good that he's here along with all the other people on this planet buzzing around the sun. Spinning…spinning…spinning.

'Jacob…wake up Jacob, the builders are here.' It's morning already with Mr Nowak's voice drifting up to the gazebo type loft. His boss sleeps on a camp bed 'downstairs' as they jokingly call the hard dirt floor at the bottom of the big shed. His wife and family of girls are living in the township nearby while the farmhouse is being built. The mallee root campfire is smouldering and Jacob soon has it hot and glowing. The billy boiling. It is his job to make a big pot of tea and cook bacon and eggs for Mr Nowak and himself.

After breakfast, Jacob is sent to fetch and carry for Tom, the builder. The men are already crawling over the house.

'How ya goin, young Jacob?' Tom yells at him from the half-built roof.

'I'm great thanks. How's ya self, Tom?' Jacob is always careful to remember names. Mum is too busy working to be around much, but what she does teach him, sticks fast. You respect everyone and give 'em a helping hand when they need it.

A stab of sorrow hits him from when he last saw his mum. Had a fancy job and a new man in her life. Barely spoke to him, as if he were not her kid at all. Told him to go find his dad. Really Mum?

'You can pass up some roofing nails, if ya like,' says Tom.

'No worries, Tom.' Jacob jumps to it, crawling up the ladder, eager to see how much work has been done on the house.

'Wow…it's gonna be pretty big,' he whispers in awe as Tom points out the big bay window in the lounge…the pantry, kitchen and breakfast room combined. Formal dining, and even a sunroom. The bedrooms shoot out at the back of the house in two wings of three and that's on top of the parents' huge bedroom with its own bathroom. Jacob wonders which room will be his.

Best of all, a lounge room fireplace almost as tall as he is. There'll be a mantel piece and fancy overmantel. Luke, one of the other workers takes a picture of Jacob's rangy figure next to it to show just how big it is. He'll have the photo developed to show Mrs Nowak when next she comes with the three girls: Suzette, Georgette and Rosie. Jacob calls them the two Ettie's and Rosie.

There's a vague notion in his head he might marry one of the Ettie's. Not Rosie, the youngest, who will find secret ways to torment him. Put gravel in his bed once and worst of all, hid his digger's hat – a gift from Uncle Joe.

Uncle Joe was the one-person Jacob could turn to when life became just too tough for words. Sent him a whole quid once. Told him to join the navy or the army and learn a trade. The only way out for people like us.

He found his digger's hat hidden on a shelf in the makeshift cold-water shower recess near the water tank with a note. It was a pencil drawing of him in the digger's hat, and he had to admit, the spitting image of him.

Rosie! He grins at the thought of her and that picture of himself she had drawn, forever safe within the pages of his only book. On the girl's next weekend visit, while the others are out riding the horses, Rosie sits at the table in the make-shift kitchen where food is prepared. She stares at the blank page before her, pencil jigging between her fingers. Her father had argued with her about a maths problem and then stormed off, telling her just to get on with it and stop dallying.

Jacob goes on with stacking dishes and wiping surfaces after the family picnic, peeping at Rosie now and then until they lock eyes, hers swelling with tears. She blinks a few times and then lays her head on folded arms against the table. From somewhere in the distance, the sound of a carolling magpie fills the air and then comes the flat toned squawk of a squeaker.

'I've heard what you tried to tell your dad,' Jacob says, 'And I know what you gotta do…it's a simple fraction. You need to find a common denominator and take one away from the other.'

'Bloody fractions…I just don't get 'em.'

'I'll do an easy one to show you how, then you can use the rule…let's say three quarters take a half.'

'That's easy enough…' Slowly they work through her problem.

'Maths,' he tells her, 'always make sense and the rules don't change.'

It's people that don't always make sense, he thinks, but you don't give up on em…yeah…you look for the good in em.

'Jacob!' Mr Nowak calls. This afternoon he will carry bricks for the brickies and timber for the carpenters. Learn a lot along the way about wiring and plumbing. About planning. A hard day ahead, but gee, soon it will be Christmas and he has a shopping trip with Mr Nowak.

He sussed out prices when last in town. With wages now owed, it should be a beaut Christmas. How quickly those days of joyful anticipation flit by, but like always things don't quite work out. When the family move in to the house, he must stay where he is in the attic of the shed.

'Makes no difference to Christmas,' Jacob says out loud to himself.

He sets traps and gets the two rats that live in the space above his head. Finds a spare ladder to use as a stairway to the roof on hot nights when he carries bedding up there and makes a night of it. From up there he sees the stars, and the Nowak's stretch of land.

If you wanted to leave it would be an hour's walk to the main road and then you'd thumb a lift to town where people come and go. You could head west from there. But what is he thinking? Christmas is coming up. Pay day and shopping. At the same time, he feels an itch that has nothing to do with his skin or any known body part. There is a question in the air.

Surely Christmas day will come with an invitation to join the family in the big house, with Rosie there to tease him or for him to tease her. Oh, how he misses her. She hasn't been near him since coming home for the holidays.

So far, his finances have worked well. He has enough money to send a ten shilling note with a card to his brother Robert in Kalgoorlie. To Uncle Joe in Perth, a nice card and a comb. They are the only addresses he has for his family. A relief in a way, cos that gives him more to spend on the Nowak's. In the general store he finds a treasure trove. For Mr and Mrs Nowak, a tiny glass dome filled with liquid. Shake it, turn it the right way up and you see snow falling over a pretty red roofed church surrounded by pine trees. For each of the Ettie's, pretty handkerchiefs and for Rosie, a tiny globe – the world on its axis.

Christmas day comes and Jacob is up and about early. He takes a cold shower and dresses in his best. Best strides, shirt and shoes polished to a sheen – dark straight hair slicked back with hair oil. A quick glance in his shaving mirror to shave that black fuzz from around his upper lip and chin.

Should he go up to the house? Or wait until they came to him? Minutes and then an hour in an agony of indecision, especially after he hears the girls chanting and singing. When they quieten down, possibly to go to the dining room for breakfast, he makes a lightening dive to leave his gifts on the front door mat.

Have they forgotten me? Jacob tries to pass the time by reading his book, but can't concentrate. His eyes keep going back to the picture Rosie drew of him and it breaks his heart. *Do I love her, is that it?* Jacob lies on his bed in the heat, wondering if he should go down to the dam in his shorts, take a swim to cool off, but then he'd have to disturb a bunch of sheep on its clay shore. Still and silent as stones they stand, while an equal lassitude creeps into his own limbs. It seems hours…a lifetime has passed when he wakens to their call. It is the Ettie's with his lunch.

A special one with a bunch of grapes and some watermelon.

Rosie has forgotten me.

'Thank you…I left…I left your presents on the front

veranda,' he tells them. Whether they answered or not he will never remember. That itch, magnified a hundredfold enters his body in waves.

When the big house stands tall and silent, when the first rays of the sun light touches the trees, spreads to the oat paddock and beyond, he is well on his way, shrugging off the heavy weight that drags at his heart. On his back, the swag lies, no heavier than it was when he arrived at the Nowak farm.

Jacob begins with no destination in mind but to be away. To put one foot after another. To look, not to the end of the journey, but to the end of his next ten steps. There'll be a bright pebble, a leaf or a dip in the road to mark the spot. Then before the next ten steps, the same, until the Nowak farm is a tiny cluster of buildings indistinguishable, one from the other.

On the open gravel road, Jacob marches to a beat, like a soldier or sailor. *Join the forces,* Uncle Joe will tell him. Learn a trade. That's a way out for people like us, but life is more than that. Look for other beginnings, other adventures. The whole world is out there. He hears a vehicle approaching and with a cheerful grin and a wave, knows that it will stop. That's all he has right now, that smile and willing hands.

'Where to?' the truckie has a Christmas hat on his head and nice light eyes. Jacob meets him with his own warm brown eyes and makes a friend for life, one of many he will meet over years.

From a distance, Rosie hears the truck stop and knows. Dear clever Jacob, you don't belong here and nor do I. You taught me that. They had banned her from spending time with the 'farm hand' and she wanted him to know it was not her doing. The note she has written slips from her left hand as she lies down on his neatly made bed. *You'll be alright Jacob and so will I, but this is my time to cry for the loss of our friendship.*

Only when her sobs abate is she conscious of the small globe – his gift to her. The world, smooth and cool in her warm hand.

28 The Touch of a Wand

When I reach the post office of our town on a certain day in 1947 at about 3.30 pm, I gasp from my run all the way from the State School. With an uneasy squelchy feeling in my tummy, I drop the weighty envelope with its see-through window into the slot marked LETTERS. That is what I was supposed to do wasn't it?

I know there is money inside and I know it is for Mr Gomme to pay for the shoes we kids need for school. Not like the days just past, when World War II still raged. We three younger siblings went bare footed to school for the most part and we were taught by our Mum who was head teacher of our little bush school. It was conveniently built near the border of our farm within a nest of stately pines and wattle. We rarely went to town. It was our dad who posted Mum's letters and brought home the mail.

Much to our sorrow our little school was torn down when the war ended and so now, here we are taken by bus to the township. I'm ten, going on eleven. Each morning we pile in with our school teacher mum. We settle for a long drive down winding gravel roads between farms on a circuitous route to our respective schools. The shorter trip in the afternoon is easier except for a regular event that sets we younger pair apart. My sister and I are 'convent dogs,' amidst a churning mass of State School kids. Our dearly loved mother, their teacher, regularly embarrasses us by sending us on missions to pick something up from the shops and then run to catch the fully loaded bus at Thomson's Corner.

'Run down the street,' she will say. 'Buy sausages and chops…oh and a pound of mince.' This, with a voice raised within the hearing of a gang of sniggering (or so we imagine) State School kids. The bus driver, she assures us, won't mind picking us up near Thompson's for the shorter route home.

When we arrive home it's shoes off, kitchen stove lit and kettle bubbling for a full pot of tea. It is served with thick slices of fresh buttered bread spread with jam and then we all settle for a quiet time with books, newspapers, journals and if we are lucky, perhaps a Phantom or Superman comic spread across the big kitchen table. This, before the nightly ritual of jobs before tea, milking dairy cows, bringing in morning wood and preparing our nightly meal.

'So, did you pay Mr Gomme?' Mum asks, as I spread more apricot jam on my bread between mighty sips of tea.

'I…I er, I posted it!' I take a bite and swallow.

'You…what?' says Mum.

'Posted it,' I say in a tiny unsure voice. Mum's usual smiley eyes are wide with alarm.

'You were supposed to give it to Mr Gomme in person…it was loose money…a lot of it…a fortnight's wage…now take your brother's bike and ride back to town.' My Mum is shaking…not exactly with rage but with a lot of strong feeling as she follows through with further instructions. I need to ask the postmaster to find that envelope and then I must pay Mr Gomme.

I'm falling off the edge of the world. I need to redeem myself. There is nothing for it but to remove myself from my mothers' gaze. Within moments I have my school shoes back on and I'm skittering down the hill from our home on my brother's rattly old bike. It is too large for me with a hard seat and that awful bar across from seat to handlebars. But I vow to do everything in my power to save myself, my family and the Gomme dynasty.

Mr Gomme, an upright man — I see in mind's eye to this day. A gentleman if ever there was one. Dressed in a pinstriped, grey suit with a waist coat, tie and hat, and in winter an umbrella in hand. He's well prepared you see whether it's actually raining or not. He will nod a polite greeting, even to a scruffily dressed girl child.

Years down the track we will all be shocked and saddened when he dies too young but cheered by the resilience of his wife and family. Within a short while his attractive wife of equal stature, can be seen smartly attired in an olive-green suit, with an umbrella to match in her hand. She is ready and willing to take over the reins of a budding business. One day the Gomme's brand name will be known far and wide.

But that is all in the future, right now, it is up to me to keep the show on the road. I pedal like crazy, red faced from the effort. I cycle over the undulating landscape. Pass one neighbour's farm and then another. Today there is no dallying at the swiftly flowing all year-round creek at Gibilinee Corner where three roads meet. With barely a glance sideways, I take a hard-left turn to face a long gradual slope, past my cousins' house where my family and I are always lovingly greeted. No such comfort today. I pedal on, my throat aching with unshed tears.

My worst moment arrives shortly after as I sense the coming of night from the looming shadows of trees nearby. Even the birds are silent except for the quick sound of their fluttering wings flying home to roost.

I must get to the post office by five, I must, I tell myself over and over, but oh dear, I hear a car coming. From the Ring Barker's meeting place by the tennis courts. I shall soon be covered in dust, coughing and sneezing until it passes. If I stop to catch my breath after that, I will lose more precious time. What if the money for our shoes has really been lost or stolen in the post? What if Mr Gomme is short of money at the end of the month and cross with my mum when his business folds? Maybe my mum will be shamed and miserable. How can I possibly get to the post office in town before five?

I don't believe in fairies or Father Christmas and I'm trying to be grown-up. I'm trying not to cry. I'm trying not to swear and curse like a boy. I wobble as the dreadful old bike squeaks along beneath me and now that car is bearing down on me. Only a fairy godmother would have the power now, to save me.

Her car passes within an inch of my body and then to my surprise, squeals to a stop. All I hear now is the tick,

tick, ticking of hot metal and then a voice. 'Would you like a lift, dear?' Enter my fairy godmother.

Her coach is square in shape with a black soft roofed canvas top. It has running boards on both sides and luckily for me, a handy gadget thing at the back on which she can hang baggage.

Short and gently rounded in stature, my fairy godmother takes charge of my bike and ushers me into her car. Short silvery waved hair frames a kindly face imbued with a soft powdery hew. She wears a touch of pink lipstick and glasses. On this day, her eyes are blue as the sky in summer. Once upon a time when I was three, she came to our door at Christmas time with presents for me and my sisters. Mine was a doll's bed made from a shoebox with a green satin frill all around it, the prettiest thing I'd ever seen.

'I'm in a tearing hurry, dear,' she says, 'I must be at the post office before five.' My fairy godmother is known throughout the district for her lateness and on this day, it works in my favour. It's like being touched by a gleaming wand and hey presto.

'Me too,' I echo, softly. Somehow this dear salt of the earth, English born fairy godmother, with her refined accent and manners, lifts my brother's rattly old bike to be attached in some way to the back of her coach. While she is thus engaged, I quickly wipe away any sign of tears.

How great is my relief when we, the last customers of the day, rush into the post office? Before I even ask for it, the kindly postmaster hands over that weird fat envelope with the money inside. A little smile plays at the corners of his lips as I dash through the door and begin to run.

With minutes to spare, I hand over the money owed to a solemn and respectful Mr Gomme who writes out a receipt for me with dignity and the utmost care. Meanwhile my fairy godmother is, 'Orff to meet friends at the golf club,' driving away from me with a little toot of her wonderful machine. She is one of two women in the district who drives a car, and the only one who runs her own farm alone.

Having been to her place for lunch one day with my mother, I remember her barn-like abode. Essentially, a single room filled with period furniture jam packed between huge unhung paintings, beautifully bound books and china-ware. All in no particular order. Her story yet to be told. I think of her as I ride home the long way…on the easier bitumen road and then along the gravel to our farm. I wonder how she gets on without a bunch of kids like me and my siblings to help her out. Then again, she is a fairy godmother with a lot of magic to draw upon.

29.1 The Mill

1920

On that overcast night, Anna waited and it came, a dirge like wail from the timber mill whistle. Not the usual summons for the workers to begin their labours, nor the signal for knock off time at night. It echoed and re-echoed above the smoking sawdust stacks, reaching to the settlement with its raw timber dwellings. An urgent sound rising above the wind song of giant hardwoods, the rustle and thump of wildlife, but more immediate and urgently, to the men on foot and horseback. They were searching for the lost man.

Two nights gone since he set out to fish for marron in the river a mile or so up stream. Anna shivered, knowing instinctively the man was dead. Surely not another suicide.

'That poor young woman,' said Mrs McLeod, shaking her head sadly while Anna prepared soup for the child-widow. Sent Rebecca with the food and freshly made damper. It was all she could do. Her own loss still too raw. Too close. Though blessed with three healthy children, another child had come. Stillborn. The midwife murmuring, 'I'm sorry Mrs Bree."

Gabe had come unwashed from his job as feller, deep in the heart of karri country, their tears mingling with wood sap as they mourned their loss. Only Gabe with his smiling blue eyes could help Anna recover. Only he could make her go on believing in their dream – to have a place of their own. A welcoming place of refuge. How they longed for it. Saved for it. Planned for it.

'If you have land, you live,' Anna would tell Rebecca. Her brave girl, just ten, with a long swathe of shining black hair and an air of moral certainty in her smiling grey-blue eyes. Just last week, with the passion and force of her words alone, Rebecca shamed a gang of bully-boys to free a dugite snake they had captured to torture.

Due to her mother's recent ill health, Rebecca became second mother to Eddie — short sighted and fearful of shadows. The little fellow was the butt of constant bullying and teasing from the snake torturing gang. He was defended vigorously by Rebecca and their younger brother, Kenny with his sold little frame and dark watchful eyes. A boy — one day to be a man who said little, but thought deeply. When he did speak, even the toughest boy or girl would listen.

Across the way from Anna and her family, Emily Broun groaned. There was somebody knocking on her door. She looked blankly at the girl, Rebecca, to be seen most days rounding up her mother's milking goats; bloody nuisances they were, too. Here she was offering a billycan of hot soup with her clipped English speech, broadening a little towards the local drawl as time went on.

Emily took the food without smiling, feeling disengaged and strange but suddenly hungry. She roused

herself enough to light the kerosene lantern and was startled to find baby Lara, lying perfectly still, with eyes wide
open staring right into hers.

'I haven't anything for you!' She cried, brokenly.
'Look, see? Nothing but a trickle in the left breast and the
right.' Oh, she was so tired, but beneath the tiredness, it
flared. Pure rage. Tim promised her the decent housing
would come later. The company manager had shown him
the plans. Four rooms and a veranda with a washhouse
and dunny out the back. A picket fence all round with a
cow-catcher at the gate.

*Should call it goat catcher. Damn things, always breaking out
of their enclosure.* Emily had seen the humour at the
time…before the baby…before…the foggy disengage-
ment that followed.

Where are you, Tim? There was water to be drawn from
the communal well. No dry bush kindling in the wood
box, the fireplace stone cold. She had wasted a bottle of
kerosene, trying to light it and ended up with a pyramid
of blackened jarrah sticks green as bloody grass. Cold air
drifted through the cracks in the walls of the slab hut.
Thrown together by Tim, as if he didn't care. In fact, he
was good with his hands. A real craftsman with wood.
She had loved those hands.

The baby's crib moved and she looked down again to
see a pair of blue green eyes flecked with darkness staring
into hers. Perfectly focussed. 'Oh baby, what am I to do
with you?' Emily's life with Timothy was all so different
from what she…what they…had hoped. If only she
hadn't felt so drained after Lara's birth, so detached and

dreary and there was that persistent cough that irritated Timothy. It seemed that he couldn't bear to be around her. Ever ready to make excuses to be away from her.

When Tim fell in love with her he'd been married to a harridan with a bunch of ungrateful brats. When he danced with Emily the attraction was instant and fierce. He didn't just love her, he worshipped her. 'You have the prettiest face I have ever seen,' he told her. He reckoned her good legs and dainty figure were a bonus. In his arms, she felt beautiful. Some said she was a tramp, but she never had been or wanted to be with anyone but Tim. A capable man, finding work was never a problem. It was just bad luck he'd married such a mean witch. Wanted to 'wear the pants' they said. Never satisfied. Emily sat down in the cane chair wrapped in a blanket with her child.

Across the lane, Gabe Bree arrived home in the early hours with the news.

'We found him face down where the river lies deep.'

Rebecca heard her parents' muffled conversation through the thick woollen blanket that divided the children's sleeping area from the kitchen. She felt like crying.

'What is it?' said Kenny, his dark eyes wide. Beside him, Eddy's weak blue eyes welled with tears.

'Oh, that little baby's daddy is dead, poor babby.'

A rush of wind stirred the vast unknowing forest. It sounded like the sea. A frogmouth hooted. A curlew cried. There were thumps of a 'roo close by and all the while after she had learned the truth, the young child-widow keening for her love. The child, too weak to cry at all.

Darkness fell. Slow and ominous over the land. Anna allowed herself a moment of nostalgia. It came so vividly; her father's sturdy home with the smell of fresh bread baked every day in the adjoining bakery. At unexpected moments she ached for the cheer and bustle of a busy household with two house-girls to do the hard work. She daren't think of that ring of mountains, with its subtle shifts of light. On a clear day, a shining band of white cloud lay below the mountain peaks that never failed to beckon. A fairy tale brightness of reassurance. What lay beyond? She wondered as a child, the end of the land itself? *How sheltered and ignorant we were.*

Anna remembered her first bleeding after her mother died. Thinking it was some kind of punishment for an imagined sin, she spent hours sitting in a bath of cold water. She looked to the African women, the progeny of slaves, upright and stately, with the weight of their burdens balanced with precision on their heads. Within a swathe of cloth, a baby or a toddler held to the breast so easily. Their voices would rise intermittently in song — operettic style, often to praise one of their own…a son's coming of age or a daughter's marriage, the rich tones redolent with the will to go on always. From slavery to servitude, yet retaining a strong sense of identity with the earth beneath their feet.

But now here Anna was, far from her roots, with nothing but a camp oven and water drawn from a communal well. Her heart ached for the wife of the lost man. The sound of her weeping came like soft rain. A young Emily Broun — the newcomer who came with a babe in arms and her man. It was said they were not married. The dead man's brother had been sent a telegram with the news. Perhaps he would come to support the mother and child. Perhaps not. Perhaps she would be left to travel back to her hometown and begin life anew…alone.

'I'll hold your baby,' Anna said at the husband's funeral, and she'd fallen in love. In love with those blue-green eyes that looked into hers so trustingly.

Within days, Anna met Emily and the baby while travelling by train to Perth. Again, she held the baby for the exhausted young mother.

'I can't…I just can't keep myself and the baby, with nobody to help me,' Emily said, with tears welling, and Anna's arms ached to hold the young mother too. The baby looked to be in the first stage of rickets…and would surely die…unless…? She needs goat milk…the best…with cream on top. A small amount often. An idea had taken route and Anna couldn't let it go. There was little time for second thoughts for either party.

'What if…what if I were to take care of her, until she grows strong and you are well enough to take care of her yourself?' Anna's heart raced as she said the words that would come back to haunt her. 'She is still your baby and you can take her back whenever you wish.'

Emily Broun moved on from Perth with the huffing and puffing of a steam engine in her ears, the smell of burning coal in her nostrils. The country on either side of the train, dry and parched between shrubs and hardy trees with bendy trunks shining like gold. Separated from

Timothy, who was buried now in that rain sodden forest. It was not her kind of place. 'Oh Timothy…'

Emily Broun moved on without fanfare or last good-byes, except for the one in her head. *Goodbye for now, Lara, my baby…but not forever…one day…I will come back for you.*

29.2 Once Upon a Time

A hush came over the little bush school as Miss Stanley began reading, and sometimes telling, the story from a book with colourful pictures. Dreamy eyed, Lara gave herself up to the words while a shaft of sunlight from the window warmed her bare arm.

Miss Stanley's story told of an orphan boy adopted by a kind woodcutter and his wife in the very old days when anything might happen…or might not happen…in which it was quite acceptable for a good fairy or an ogre to cross the path of a child like herself.

The mill whistle blew, signalling a stoppage of some kind and Lara came to herself as if waking from a dream.

'The woodcutter,' Miss Stanley explained, 'looks a little like Lara's dad don't you think?'

She stared at the picture as her teacher held up the page. 'It does look like my dad,' Lara said, with a flush of pleasure. She was so proud of her dad. He was tall but not too tall, with smiley blue eyes and he was clever. People came to him when they wanted to write an important letter. It helped that he had studied law, before he and mum migrated to Western Australia. They said he was 'educated.' But he was kind too, and people loved him for it. The woodcutter in the story even had the same golden tinged hair and a moustache like her dad.

'He is like your dad,' said Valerie, her best friend.

'Yes,' said Tricia, 'and you are like the boy.'

'But I'm not a boy. I'm a girl with red hair. That boy has black hair and he looks Chinese.'

'You are like him. You are just like him.'

'No!'

'Yes.'

'No,' Lara cried, flushed and angry.

'That boy wasn't really the woodcutter's kid, he was adopted and so were you,' Tricia said, smugly.

'I am not.'

'You are.'

'I am not, am I Miss Stanley?'

With no warning at all, the world turned upside down. The sky floated under her feet and the heavy dark earth hung over her. Air squeezed out of her lungs. Her blood ran cold and she leapt out of her seat and ran…out of the door, away from Tricia, away from the other children's shocked faces, but most of all, from what she saw in Miss Stanley's eyes.

Lara cut along on the path by the mill, past smouldering sawdust stacks and heaped logs with bark stripped clean from the trunks. The fallen trees looked scarred and sad, just like she felt. In a defiant gesture she chose the long way home to the farm down the twisty gravel road. It didn't matter that Kenny would be waiting for her with Laddie to take her home through the shorter bush track.

On winter days like this he would be ready to help her climb onto the back of their big friendly draft horse. Lara would nestle into Kenny's warm back, loving the slightly damp smell of horse and the forest litter kicked up by Laddie's hoofs. Lara knew every tree. Every fallen log and what birds inhabited which tree.

'Kenny's not my real brother,' she blubbered, sniffing back a flood of tears. The thought of his broad kind face looking worried at her absence, was a knife plunging into her heart. *You're not my brother and nor is Eddie. Eddie* — so protective and fearful for her safety. 'Watch out for snakes coming home the long way.' His warnings ran in her head. 'The tiger snakes are worst, especially when nesting.'

It was Rebecca who taught her not to be fearful, just to watch where you tread and wait if you see one. The snake will be scared too and soon slide away. Her big sister was brave as Queen Boadicea who fought the invading Romans in East Anglia. In the 'motherland', Dad said.

'Not my motherland,' Mum would say. 'She's no friend of mine.' Then her solemn face would be calm with a little smile on her lips. 'But she gave me your daddy. Now let's put the kettle on and we'll warm our feet on the open oven door.' And the two of them would sit with Mum telling stories about far away Africa where she taught little black kids to read and about the long, long journey some of her countrymen made by wagon. Was that a lie too?

The sky darkened and fat sploshes of rain hit her face. *I don't care if I'm soaked to the skin.* Her warm winter coat was still on its peg at school marked with her name, 'Lara Bree'. Was that her real name? The sploshes turned to a torrent, pelting on and around her. The trees swayed, reaching out with their limbs as if wanting to be free of the earth that bound them. It made her think of the sea, the rush and the roar. Seen only twice in her life at Windy Harbour. It scared her but thrilled her too. So, what if a tree did drop a limb on her? Wouldn't they all be sorry then? Sorry about her being ADOPTED. Why had they lied to her?

'I am not the fruit of your womb,' she wanted to scream at her mum. The words came from a prayer to Holy Mary, her Catholic friend, Valerie taught her. As Lara approached the home farm, she saw Dad raking up rubbish in the yard. Part of her wanted to run to him, cry…crying like a mad dingo under the moon. How could her beautiful Daddy, not be her real one? Today he looked older, more bent than usual. As if he knew something terrible had happened. Unable to face him, she scampered past and ran to the back of the house.

The girls' room was her refuge, with the wooden bed and a drawer set painted, by the boys, a glossy pale green for her birthday because that was her favourite colour. Mum made her a quilt to match, saving the soft down of poultry for a year to stuff it. Shivering, Lara crawled under. She hadn't eaten since lunch and was hungry but could not face her mum or anyone.

The house seemed too empty and too quiet, except for the delicious savoury smell of soup and the steady hum of the iron kettle on the hob of the stove. The soup would be rich and satisfying with a medley of baby carrots and other vegetables from those put aside during the thinning process in the garden. It was a job she liked to do for Mum to save her troublesome leg. The leg that made her lame. Lara wagged school more than she should, pretending to have a tummy ache just to be home with Mum and Dad.

'You give into that child, too easily,' Mrs Kenny, a teacher friend, once said in her hearing. Partly with relief and a surge of fresh anger, she wanted to know what the family were saying.

'She's home,' Dad said. 'She's safe…that's what matters right now.'

Gabe Bree's mind flicked back to when Lara was three years old, perhaps a little older. No word from the mother until then, but it was time. Emily had married and wanted her child.

In the fret of tears and anguish that followed, the tiny girl tried to comfort each member of the Bree family with hugs, kisses and lisped words of comfort.

'Don't c'y,' Becky. Don't c'y,' with a heart-breaking sweetness that fuelled more tears.

During a sleepless night, Abe decided.

'We'll fight this, Anna.'

Drawing on his knowledge of law, Gabe stated their case to the authorities, concentrating on what he and Anna could do to provide for Lara: the home block they owned, the number of goats in their herd, the income he had from his service pension, a block of land in the city owned by Anna. Yet all the while he knew it had nothing to do with what they owned. They had simply fallen in love with this child.

'Something has upset Lara,' he said. 'Maybe somebody at school said something.'

'Yes…I'll make tea.' Anna was too upset to respond properly. She wanted to smooth away his worry lines but her back ached, and there was so much to do.

'Fetch the goats for milking,' she snapped at the boys in her stern voice, reminding them to feed oats to Laddie and be sure to shut the gates along the way. She confronted Lara, standing at the bedroom door. 'As for you, Miss, we were worried sick. Now change out of your wet clothes or you'll catch your death of a cold.'

Lara choked on words she wanted to scream. *You are not my mother!* She saw Mum through a blur of bitter tears recalling the warm soft mother she loved best when she spoke with longing about South Africa or when she might sing the comforting hymn. *When he cometh, when he cometh to make up his jewels. Precious jewels, precious jewels, his love and his own.* At such times Lara felt like a precious jewel herself just from the expression in Mum's eyes. Like the stars of the morning…But Mum was no longer her mum and Dad, no longer her dad. Looking out of the window she saw Dad's head and shoulders above the sunflowers by the gate and it broke her heart. Blindly, she dashed past Mum and ran from the house, across the paddock down by the creek.

It was Rebecca who found her. Rebecca who wrapped her in a woolly blanket and held her with those words of comfort. 'We all love you, Lara.'

At teatime, Mum gave her the shank from the soup.

It was a privilege. Something you were given when you needed building up after an illness. An act of love.

Yes…they do love me, she thought, but a voice in her head told her, one day I will find my real mother. I must, because I'm the fruit of her womb. *But why? Why did you give me away?*

29.3 Emily's Choice

As the fierce sun dips behind the mine head, Emily places her smoothing iron on the stove top. She eases her aching back to stand at the open back door of Louise's washhouse, taking in a whiff of cool air. It is that time of day in the summer of 1936 when the Great Boulder Gold Mine, with its pyramid mine heads and chimney stacks, is awash in a golden-red glow. Even the enclosed cyanide tanks and supporting structures are bathed at the edges in the flickering rosy light.

From the shanty town on the nearby flats Emily is soothed by the hum of homely things. The stoking of campfires, the lighting of lamps, the savoury smell of cooked food. And then afterwards the mellow beauty of men's voices raised in song. It is the Italians workers imported by the esteemed Mr Hoover. The low cost of their labour will make him a rich man and the locals angry. But for Emily, their song takes her right away, imbued as it is with love and longing…for absent wives, children, extended families and the centuries old culture and customs of Italy.

Emily recalls earlier in the day, a familiar swirl of red dust, the rattle of metal wheels and harrumphing of camels that herald the arrival of the tall rangy Afghan. Comes with his cart load of goods for sale. Dirndl frocks for little girls, dried fruits, edible seeds, medicines and nick-knacks. Emily had savoured the mixed-up smells while the man offered a gift of sweet meats.

'For your boy,' he said, with a warm glint of humour in his dark eyes. She vows to hold the memory close, a reminder of the innocence and wonder of childhood. Where is that gutsy little girl she had been and once knew? Emily wonders as the world closes in on her and her chest tightens.

'I have bought something for Danny,' she calls to Louise who is dampening down somebody's best shirt before ironing it for tonight's dance.

With a familiar rush of anticipation, Emily feels the excitement that makes Saturday night special. It out-weighs the cringeworthy feeling of being a deserted wife. There is very little money to spare but she has a bought a few treasures for herself and Danny. A pretty thing for herself and for her boy, a pocketknife housed in a leather pouch decorated with the Afghan Dari symbol. As she stashes away her purchases, her own image in Louise's hallstand mirror, mocks — two flushed cheeks and blue-green eyes — tell–tale eyes. *How long can I keep it from Louise when it has taken me so long to admit it to myself?*

Emily loves that Danny goes to school every day and is well past the age that she was taken away from school to help mother at home, such as it was. Always in crisis. She wants more for him than she ever had. A job that he loves. A real home.

Last night, before leaving him with Len's mum, she told him, 'Danny…you have a sister…and one day you will find her…or she will find you.'

Emily's thoughts come without words. Her unvoiced knowledge deeply felt. One loss on another; her young sister lost to diphtheria, still with that sweet nutty smell of baby about her head. *To the river of no return*, her dad would say. Emily's childhood loss remains. Her little sister, still a child who once lived and breathed like Danny. Never again to feel the homely warmth of a kitchen stove, the coolness of tree shade, or safety under blankets when rain pelts down on the roof above. Never to laugh or cry or know the comfort of shared love, joy or sorrow.

And her first love, Timothy — buried in the far southwest within a forest tossed by wind with a sound like the sea, forever shedding coats of bark with ominous thumps. *I never wanted that for you.*

After Timothy's death, Len had come into Emily's life. At first, he was protective of her and in love. In return, Emily loved being a 'wife'. A real wife this time round, with a ring on her finger, married to a gold miner with a steady job. There was a sense of pride in that. The tucker box she prepared for him always the best, with a sweet treat slipped in beside sandwiches and fruit whenever she could manage it. Even if she and Danny did without, as breadwinner, his needs were sacrosanct.

In the early days of their marriage, Len shared his day with her, making her laugh or feel sorry for some 'idiot' who broke the rules and ended up injured or sacked. She wanted to know every detail. From when the men gathered in the space they called *the dry* where they changed into working clothes, to the day's end. Emily laughed when Len mimicked Freddy Bent's throat clearing and the grunts that passed as a kind of greeting in the morning. And the mean fisted little despot who handed out candles — strictly one per miner and God help you if you asked for an extra.

Len would tell her how he teamed up with four or five mates to share the ride on the metal seat of a cradle to descend the pit. You'd loosen up a bit and share a joke or take the mickey out of Sid whose wife was pregnant again. Before you know it, you are a mile down into a dense blackness you could never imagine until you experienced it yourself. The men's descent ends in a cavern like space with solid pillars of untouched earth and rock, left standing to keep it stable. The space they call "the room" is big enough for trolleys on rails to hold the ore and other equipment, even a horse — poor thing kept down there — a life sentence she's told. Within the room, walls, roof and entries to each 'lode' are shored up with hard woods from the southwest and local timbers like mulga and gimlet. Emily knows them by heart.

Sometimes she dreams of that place. Of Len, young enough and fit enough to climb to his lode on an upper level above Freddie Bent's. Wedged behind a small stone in the wall, Len's single candle flickers and flares in a constant dance, sending ghost shadows through a haze of fine dust particles into the musty air. He labours with pick and shovel, hacking out ore. To be conveyed to the surface in a trolley. A ceaseless grind of steam powered mobility. The ore in exchange for life giving air pumped into the fug deep in the earth.

At tucker time, Len guzzles from his water bag and then bites into sandwiches hungrily. He is voiceless until energy seeps back into his bones. Only then can he nod to a mate, grumble about the water seepage that turns the ground under their feet to mush that day, or notice young Harris has grown a beard, opening himself to jocular teasing by workmates.

As Louise says, 'Len is like most of those guys, they grumble about bloody foreigners or a toff who thinks he's better than anyone else, but never discuss things that are close to their hearts.' Yet at her loneliest — before Louise and Molly became her lifelong friends — Emily envied the comradery between working men.

Gold is a quirk of nature, Emily sees that now, a weird thing you can't eat or even use, except as jewellery or as a measure for money. She learns later, there are other uses for it, but at what cost? Emily gags to think of the sodden ground and fusty air Len endures each day. Yet she knows he still goes on, never counting the cost yet knowing that many workmates will die by accident or the onset of lung disease.

Look after the breadwinner her elders advise. Even Molly, who runs her own boarding house and pub. During those few short years with Len, Emily had pride in taking care of 'her man'. A nice cup of tea when he landed home at night and a hearty meal to follow. Danny knew not to touch those special biscuits for Dad's tucker box. After two cups of tea, Len 'popped into the pub, for a beer with the boys' coming home either full of ardour or irritability. He couldn't cope with a crying child. 'Shut that kid up,' he yelled, more and more as his ardour waned and drinking increased.

'Daddy works very hard and he needs his sleep.' Emily lay beside the little boy, rubbing his back to sooth him to sleep.

'He needs a good clout,' Len muttered before deep sighs of exasperation.

How can a clout ever be good? Emily held back her anger or wept quietly, unable to find the words or a sensible argument. She was almost relieved when Len slept over at his mum's house and then, one day, he didn't come home at all.

She will rest today and dance tonight. Emily brushes away thoughts of that stern doctor's warning. Brushes away thoughts of that place — the long rows of hospital beds on the veranda. 'For the fresh air,' they said.

When she returns to her own place after working with Louise all day, Emily opens up the windows to let cool night air into her house, a glorified hut with whitewashed hessian walls. It looked grand in her eyes with a small fringe of garden and neat as a new pin inside. The red bougainvillea at the front is blooming and so is the sweet-scented slip of honeysuckle she has been coaxing along, keeping it moist with dishwater all summer.

Washing the filthy clothes of gold miners and ironing their 'best' is back breaking work, but working in partnership with Louise, has come with the gift of friendship. Real friendship with a kind of understanding she has never experienced before. Molly too, is an affectionate elder in her life, bringing wisdom and balance. It was

Molly who helped her come to terms with the disappointment of losing custody of Lara.

Tears brim Emily's eyes when she remembers feeling so alone and lost, wondering what the future held for her and her boy…taking up a pen, writing a letter to her daughter…a big girl now, she was sure…yet knowing her words hardly made sense. As if she were splattering her pain across the page. Swearing stupidly in between tears afterwards, cursing her lack of schooling and sense of being not good enough.

Let it go, Emily tells herself, *you tried to get your daughter back and you failed.*

She looks out at the 'stacks' of hardened slag heaps beyond the mine head. It is where Danny and his friends like to play, scrambling up and down, shooting at pigeons with their gings. Emily smiles at the memory of a day just past when Danny and a friend offered to help her wash clothes. Stomping on the coloureds soaking in the tub with their bare feet, they sang at the top of their voices. *'This is the way we wash our clothes, wash our clothes, wash our clothes, this is the way we wash our clothes all on a Monday morning.'*

Oh Danny…what will become of us? Gold…gold mines tunnelling under the red dirt. Is that where you will work too? After mining, a landscape, bare as the moon. Yet this is still Emily's place. Danny's too. On rare occasions they will take time out with Louise and Molly to explore bushland nearby with those trees with smooth golden trunks beneath a crumbled outer bark. Sometimes in the crackling dry of summer, a racehorse goanna, a startling figure, still as a fallen twig one moment and in the next a moving stream. Fleet footed and swift as a bird with wings. These are the images Emily holds in her mind's eye. Precious images of life. Her life as it wobbles like broken reflections on a lake. Like that of her young sister all those years ago.

1935 with two marriages behind her. Two children…Danny and the absent Lara. Emily tries not to linger on the memory of her deep depression before and after Tim's death. The long journey by train from Perth to Kalgoorlie with the smell of burning coal, the whoosh of air as the train spun with such assurance and vigour through the wilderness and the regular beat of its message to prick her…like needles. *You gave her away…gave her away…'*

But not forever, her heart cried. *I didn't mean forever.*

From her arms into somebody older…somebody wiser in the way of babies…Lara so fragile and so…unknowable. Yes, Lara might have died without Mrs Bree's intervention. Emily knows that now.

And after the official letter informing her about the 'best interests of the child…'

Oh yes, tonight she will dance.

Everything is in place. The sheen of her dark green dress is a perfect contrast against her reddish-brown hair cut by Louise into a fashionable bob. A touch of rouge on her pale cheeks and the faintest trace of lipstick. And then her dancing shoes, each one decorated with a black voile daisy bought from the Afghan. The heel, a genuine 'dancing heel' neither too high nor too flat. Tonight, she will dance the Kalgoorlie Quickstep, the Charleston and everything in between.

Emily has taken the Afghan's medicine. Her eyes are bright and blue-green like the real sea. She will dance tonight.

'So, you saw the doctor?' Louise asked.

'I was so busy today…and I needed to take Danny to Len's mum…I bought cough mixture from the Afghan…' She pivots around and the bottom frill of her green dress flares. Pretty legs. Pretty feet pivoting.

The tiny spot of blood on her handkerchief might have come from her nose. In fact, Emily is sure it did come from her nose, after all. The fool of a doctor doesn't know what he's talking about. They say he drinks.

'Don't look at me like that, Louise…and don't you dare breathe a word to Molly, you know what she's like.'

Tonight, she will dance and she does. She dances with the Italian boy who doesn't speak a word of English. She dances with the stranger who has music in his bones. He always chooses her for the fast-moving Kalgoorlie Quick Step. Every man in the hall loves this Emily, with her sparkling eyes, her rosy cheeks, and dancing feet. She is everyman's dream yet belongs to nobody. She is Emily who lives fully and will die young.

Louise and Molly are there to pick her up when she falls, when a massive bleed takes her away from them. Emily succumbs to the disease, tuberculosis, and dies at the age of forty with her son and friends, Louise and Molly at her side. Unbeknown to her, it is the same year that her daughter, Lara marries a man with mischievous laughing eyes and the voice of an angel.

Many years pass before Danny makes an important connection with his sister and her children, a son and three daughters who welcome a greater sense of identity and continuity that knowledge can bring.

As an old lady, Lara never quite forgives her birth mother for 'giving me away' but looks with pride at her maternal heritage, pointing out the likeness between herself and other family members. At the same time, the central point in her sitting room is a professional photograph of her adoptive father, Gabe. *My real father.*

30. Underside 2015

On this night she dreams of a place in the sun and then wakens to another day in the dark house. Dampness has spotted the walls and the ceiling sags from the weight of a once elaborate light fitting. She pushes back the bed covers and lights a candle. From a distance she hears the sound of an early morning train heading out of Perth Central for the Fremantle run. When she lifts a sheet of iron from a gap in the wall, a draft of cold air hits her. It is mid-winter and this is a city of strangers. Another day in which she must survive. She will wash in cold water in a public toilet and dress carefully. Grateful for a smile from a stranger, she enjoys the attention of the old people on their way to attend a cosy community centre for the aged where you're likely to meet a friendly face.

She offers you her name — Sylvia, and will make up stories that will please you. Yes, a student. I'm studying sociology. Or it might be, I'm doing accountancy…yes, it's a good career path. Ballet? Words like arabesque, barre, allegro and chasse come easily. My agent is scouting for a part in a West Australian production as we speak. Ballet is so demanding and I need a place where I can practise my moves. Outside, the street people are stirring.

The hollow-eyed woman is awake. 'So…What

happened to you last night, Sylvia? Thought you'd be on the street with the rest of us.'

'I…Found somewhere…a shelter…'

'Not the old dump that is due for demolition? Been there, done that. Full of used needles and crap. You should have stayed here with us. At least its clean and we get a cup of soup from the Salvo's most mornings.'

There's a less up-front man who does very well for himself without the humiliation of asking for a handout. Mr Events Man dresses in a suit and tie. On this stormy winter night, he attends a Book Award event in the State Library. Drinks and nibbles are set out on tables. Easy pickings for our man. But tonight, something is wrong. His glass of red is okay but the food, not up to scratch. He takes a scrap of something on a biscuit, shaking his head, remembering the good old days when they served up food you could get your teeth into. A fat sausage roll, nice meaty mini pie or a decent ham sandwich. Tonight, he's unsatisfied and uneasy. People are arriving and as usual there's an excess of aeroplane hugs and congratulatory greetings.

Oh darling…a book of poetry? That's marvellous…I think it's an Eastern Stater who's up for the award this year…no surprises…

A snooty woman official is eyeing our events man.

My wife loves blue books…oh that's so funny, but so do I…

Conversations buzz around him.

'I think they're on to me, the fuckwits…' Mr Events Man mutters but still he sips wine and eats. He smiles and nods a lot. Usually people feel easy in his company without conversation, more interested in talking than listening, but tonight the woman official in high heeled shoes and tight black skirt eyes him again before whispering about him to the boss lady.

'Get rid of him,' Boss Lady hisses in reply.

He's almost had enough anyway. They can stick it up themselves for all he cares. He waits for a fresh crowd of people to come in and then slips past the officials, through to the 'Gentlemen's' and out the other way. In the cloak room he switches his own coat from the op shop for a pure woollen jacket. He knows all the good brands, oh yes, he does. No flies on him. Not like the naïve rough sleepers setting up their beds under the eaves outside the library. Suffice to say that he'll be warm tonight.

Meanwhile the night goes on within the library with well-practised speakers – the State Premier, publishers, editors and authors. Even our man knows it takes a damn lot of grit to write a book. Words and more words tinged with a studied mix of humility and pride while outside a drama is coming to a climax.

The central character is a woman, a nameless regular among the rough sleepers who have chosen to sleep under the overhang of the city library roof. On the northeastern side away from the worst of the wildest, wettest and coldest June night on record. It is embarrassingly close to the back exit seen by those invited guests who pick up a taxi or catch an arranged lift home.

Get rid of those rough sleepers, the doorman has been told between gusts of howling wind, rain and hail. A heated argument goes on between the doorman and the woman, their words drowned by another downpour and then in that pause, always a shock, the moment is so utterly soundless — then inside that silence a woman's voice. Clear and bell like, it rises from the darkness. More eloquent and more compelling than any other pronouncement heard that night.

'We have permission to stay here. We homeless people have a right. I've spoken to the Chief Executive Officer at the shire. You cannot send us away! You cannot!'

Another gust of rain and hail hits and then in the lull, a warm body of well-coated people rush for the exits and her words are drowned.

31 An Artist is Born

He stays until the fishing fleet spreads out across the water, like blobs of flotsam dipping one by one below the horizon line. Straddling his bicycle, a leggy pre-adolescent boy stares at the empty sea. This may have been the moment a dream was born and then forgotten: to make a boat and sail away — into those deep blue troughs of the sea and then to rise on the swell with white wings spread.

The rumble of traffic brings him back and he remembers home…the horses. Anxious now, more anxious than any child should be, he leaps into action, pedalling furiously, wanting, in spite of a growing sense of defiance, to prevent his father from yelling at him before the day has even begun.

Today, Saturday, is reserved for the exacting, age-old science of making horseshoes. When the boy turned five, his father told him, 'Now you will work and you'll do as you're bloody well told.'

He is older now and knows not to question. The father is a member of the historic Fremantle trotting fraternity. Horses are his business. A hard-headed survivor, he's clever with his hands and unscrupulous in coercing others to work. Among the father's innovations is a forge made with a forty-four-gallon drum and fitted with a handle for the blower. In between striking the hot metal with a sledge-hammer, it is the boy's task to turn the handle of the blower to heat the metal.

'Faster, turn that bloody handle faster,' the father shouts. Amidst the high-pitched screeches emitted by the blower, the boy blinks away sooty dust from his eyes, feels the weight of the breathless air, smoke laden and heavy with the mixed-up smells of horse dung, coke dust and burning metal. As the father's gaze burns into his, the boy flinches at the inexplicable rage he sees.

'You lazy good for nothing, I said turn it faster.' Faster…faster…spin the world faster…show an impassive face…let the words slide away…

On this day, while the father is out of sight, working on the final stages of the job, the boy turns the handle once more in an effort to please. The first time it is a genuine mistake, and then of its own volition, the banshee in his head screams — *faster, faster. Let the world spin. Let the flames leap higher and higher. Hotter and hotter. Let those metal horseshoes hiss and glow with sparkles of scarlet, orange, gold* — brilliant colours melting and melding.

Exhilarated, the boy faces screamed abuse with a sense of deep satisfaction. While the father slings away the molten mass, he affects the humble 'dumb' look expected of him, all the while whispering to himself, 'You did say to turn the handle faster.'

In the cold ashes of the fire, the boy will find a magical something that will sustain him until the end of his days. From that moment, he willingly faces his father's wrath to repeat the miracle of creation. That first crude sculpture along with others is carefully retrieved from the coke ash and hidden under his bed. He cannot know the future in which, with paint brush and watercolours, he will make the flowers and grasses of the desert dance. Nor can he possibly understand the creative impulse that will guide him to create beautiful objects — sculptures in metal and gleaming furniture made from the native timbers of his country.[3]

---

[3] Extract from the profile of Artist and Sculptor, Kevan Collet by the author.

32 Wings

Alana finds her way to the hospital café in Mount Street and into a haze of smoke-filled light. It is God knows what hour past midnight. From a device somewhere, a saxophonist plays the old tunes. At the counter a Vietnamese boy smiles broadly and she orders a double shot of coffee. Intimate conversations hum around her. Whiffs of another woman's grief. It is all about bodily parts and function. The gut, the liver, the heart. The heart of the matter.

The coffee is bitter on her tongue. Alana escapes to stand on the street. A taxi is impossible to call at this hour and so she walks towards Hay Street. A young couple passes. They're holding hands, she, tottering on high heels. *Lionel, it might have been you and me as we were so long ago.* Me in those impossible heels. Impossible dreams. Each of us.

A nesting bird calls from the reeds in the small nature park across from the hospital. A frightened call. A mother is guarding her young. *That's what mothers do, Lionel. Guard their brood from hurt. Rather than attacking, we will persuade and appease to keep the peace.*

Feed the prickly beast. There's no getting away from it, he is you in an ugly mood after drinking with the pub crowd. You would see one child as villain, hurtling angry words. Always one, sent to bed in tears. A scapegoat for your insecurities with misdirected angst. A door left open. A light switch left on. A persistent cough in the night (unforgiveable – that one).

By some miracle Alana knows their forgiving children are here for them now, offering her a home away from home. No questions.

Alana walks quickly and then in the darkest street, runs with a tinge of fear at her back. Runs in her sensible shoes. She has learned…those spiked heels — a death trap.

Once he called out after some remark she had made. 'Alana, you're just an old duck who doesn't know any-thing.' There were guests. Two of his boyhood friends and rivals. He was proud of his quick tongue.

Alana replied with a flippant laugh, 'Ah yes…but the duck has an emerald wing.' She watches those little brown ducks every day, floating quietly on the river. Still as statues. Once startled, they rise as one with flashes of emerald green. And then transform into sleek black curves flying in synchronicity above the water.

In Hay Street, Alana reaches the end of the enclosed walkway that leads her to a line of waiting cabs. Breath-less, she signals the nearest one. A few hours of rest at their son's house and another day awaits. Alana masks her sadness behind dark glasses believing that to share her grief might twist it somehow into a half-truth or leave her naked. She cries for Lionel and herself. Cries for be-ing with him but without him for so very long. Cries because he didn't really see her, know their children, or recognise family love when he might have held it in his hands.

Is this forgiveness? This? This woman running to the hospital like some kind of crazed banshee? She is there to look out for him. Is this love? Sinking to the floor when he screams for her to tell the doctor to let him die? Wanting to fall right into the floor and die herself. She didn't imagine that terrible red gash from the top of his thorax to the bottom would ever heal, that either of them would ever laugh again. In that moment, the husband of another patient appears from a nearby room to hold her. He leads her to the seat she will dub the "crying couch". Dark brown leather, elaborately padded. She imagines it came from some board room full of serious, upright men.

'I saw you…' The man is not much taller than her. His hazel eyes are kind. In a thick Italian accent, he tells her. 'Your husband…he be okay.' His wife is in post-operative care after surgery too. He shrugs. Grins. 'All the time, she say, 'I wanna my bed raised up.' I put it up, she wanna it down. I put it down, she wanna it up. She wanna da flowers. I give her flowers, Now she no wanna da flowers.'

Alana writes out her heart's misery on scraps of paper as her husband's body is wracked by a Golden Staph infection. She finds him one morning, half naked and soiled, sprawled across the hospital bed, cushioned with pillows the nurse has used to stop him bashing his infected legs against the metal enclosure. When she bends to help the nurses with his care, he fixes her with his inimitable glare. For a moment he is the indomitable head man, the one in charge. Father, husband, workplace boss, the one who approves or disapproves. Love and esteem are not for the unworthy. He shakes his head vehemently.

'Not you.'

She walks away. Anywhere. Nowhere. Finds herself on a footbridge overlooking a ribbon of traffic weaving towards Riverside Drive. In each car, a person in a family. Where are they going? *Where in God's name are we going, Lionel?* Yet like a homing pigeon, she returns to the unresolved. For the first time in days, he is with her and understands exactly the depth and gravity of the moment for his future wellbeing.

'Do you want me to leave?' she asks.

'No…please stay.'

She grits her teeth for the long haul, images and words resounding in her head. Their eldest son telling her, 'I have just signed Dad's leg away.' And their eldest daughter, 'Dad thought you were there until he saw you walk through a wall.' And Lionel in his delirium with his phantom legs (he had lost the other by then), ordering their son-in law to give him a hand up. He wants to put on his shoes and have a beer with the boys — their sons and sons-in-law.

She sees those soft leather shoes in her mind's eye, with a faint imprint of his long narrow feet and echoes of their athletic stride. She has an impression too, of his indomitable presence and its impact on their children, countless students and younger colleagues, all of whom hungered for his approval and esteem.

He liked to fix things and get things done. With a certain largess he willingly rescued 'idiots' who got themselves bogged in quicksand. He liked to 'run a tight ship'. As their sons will say, 'His knots never came undone.'

She is told that elderly patients with brain disfunction maybe be aggressive. Not Lionel. As if that outer shell, both prickly and dense, has been shed. Beneath it, she sees that vulnerable "someone" glimpsed in the effusive and persuasive lover, when they first met. It was that person who kept her in there.

Fast forward and she sees the athlete, neat. He is a natural when it comes to handling a wheelchair. With the help of a brilliant occupational therapist and physiotherapist, she learns to use a silk cloth over a board to do bed to chair and chair back to bed transfers. After he moves to the nursing home near their home, she insists on doing away with a catheter as soon as possible and establishing a near to normal bathroom routine. Logical arguments to put to a resisting head nurse and some staff members.

Alana is there for him when he arrives at the home, gaunt of face, chiselled features starkly white. Eyes wide and fearful. There are many battles to be won, but in time, there is an easier passage for him. Dark and light days passing in equal measure. She is told the nurses still call the room he was allocated, Lionel's room. One afternoon when the last ray of sunlight streams through the window, she prepares to leave for home when he grabs her hand to hold her back.

'I love you.' He says the simple words he found so hard to say to anyone and then he goes on, 'I fell in love with you. I fell in love with you twice.' Now his face clouds over. 'Was there another…Alana…?' His wife says nothing but recalls that woman. A colleague of his but that was in another life. He was an attractive older man, ardent when in love. Perhaps he thought it okay to kiss her in his wife's presence. Or, though his eyes saw her, his mind skipped over her. Smitten as he was. She had been warned by one of his staff.

'Be careful of that,' she said. That other Alana was leaving. Everyone was leaving. It was the end of the year with a turnover of staff. All a little drunk and singing that song about leaving on a jet plane.

'I love you,' he says the words again. In the early hours of the next morning, he phones his wife from the nursing home. He is distressed and crying. Repeating the words over and over. 'I'm sorry…I'm so sorry…I've been away all night…I went off without giving you a thought. I'm so sorry.'

'You've had a bad dream…'

'But I left you alone.'

'It's all right, I forgive you…I forgive you. I'll be there, first thing in the morning. Are you cold? Can you call the night nurse?'

One day after a visit from their children and grand-children, Lionel takes her hand with sense of urgency. 'We were good parents, weren't we?'

'We did our best and…our children are good parents.' Alana smiles. What else can she say? At the end of his life span, in spite of chest pain and increasing confusion and stress, he never loses sight of who she is or each one of their children. From the hospital, she sees that he sees, the faces of their children with a look of recognition and then at her, still clinging to her hand. Alana holds her own breath, unconsciously following each nuance and uncertainty of his.

They speak of the death rattle and it's true then she finds, like an unwanted guest on a sunlit day, stalking in corridors where nurses come and go. Their footsteps hurrying, like soldiers in defeat. He clings to her hand, his eyes searching the faces of their children and then hers.

On this day of his dying, she would have a sail unleashed, while he, she, they, might dance to the same wind tune, in the same wave and sky time. When they might open themselves to the softness in steel, in concrete, in rock. In the unbending core of resistance. All would bend, all matter, all being as one.

33 Moments

After the party he wants to share the joy.

'Where are you leading us, brother? It's so damned cold…and dark…we're only doing this because we love you…and it's your birthday…listen to those waves…even upriver they're wild tonight…'

The bitter wind penetrates the thin stuff of his shirt. The dress shirt he wore to their dad's funeral, the last time they had all been in one place together.

He hears the mingled laughter and complaints as he leads his siblings and their partners to the place that had moved him so deeply. One night he had discovered it by chance. Now as they walk away from the glitz and the noise of the party, he remembers that kind of beauty you absorb through your skin and your gut. The sound of a leaping fish in the stillness, the thrum of oars as the canoeist passes. On that night, the opalescent moon casting its spell.

They are all in evening attire, his sisters in high heeled shoes. His words are slightly slurred. He drank too much wine.

'You'll love it…it's worth the pain. You all know the rules. No pain…no gain…and you've had too much to drink…we all have…that's why we need to clear our heads. Here Mum, take my hand…this is your kind of place.'

Are we there yet? They come to a standstill around him.

'Stop winging, you lot. Look! See! The glimmer of waves coming close…across the strip of land…and see there.'

The wind gusts in icy swirls. There is no light except from one or two mobiles. He moves on and they scramble after him along a narrow path between rocks and abutments of turf, to a strip of land that divides the waters of the bay. Waves rush in. They watch the moon coming out from the clouds with mirror images in the waters below, splintering into slivers of gold in coiling streams. They are mesmerised when, on the gnarly branch of an overhanging paperbark, a cormorant suddenly appears, a moving black sculpture straightening its curved neck to dive. A fish leaps in a maelstrom of moon dappled light.

He remembers when they swam weightless in the river near their home, dived from tree branches, and rowed upstream in the long Canadian canoe of Avon Descent fame. How time slipped through their fingers.

We are all here, he thinks. This is a moment…and don't we all know? You only have moments.

The End

Acknowledgements

I would like to say a special thanks to my daughter, Sari Smith, for all her sensitive and insightful editing of the most difficult stories in here. Also, to my daughter, Deirdre for always listening. Her impeccable knowledge of the English language and usage is a boon!

On the wider home front, thank you to my large extended family for their loyal support, to the Milli Milli writers and to my friends, Lyn Gornal and June Thompson.

Finally, thank you to Ian Hooper and all the staff at Leschenault Press for their ongoing support of local and independent authors, their attention to detail and especially to their amazing cover designer, Brittany Wilson. I simply love what she did with the outline brief I gave her.

About the Author

Helene Smith was raised in the rural area of Linfarn, Manjimup, Western Australia. Her schoolteacher mother handed on a love of literature and a tradition of storytelling which became a lifelong passion.

After a short nursing career, Helene married a schoolteacher and raised a large family, whilst all the time writing 'covertly' as a young mother – short fiction, private journal writing and poetry, honing her craft through TAFE correspondence courses. After studying Education and English and obtaining a degree as a mature student at Edith Cowan University in Bunbury, Western Australia, she wrote her first book; *Operation Clancy* (1994) inspired by a wish to produce an 'easy to read' thriller for reluctant older readers.

Since then, the sheer joy of invention and a fascination with the writing process has seen Helen produce a number of other titles.

An experienced presenter and writer/facilitator in schools, community centres and institutions for adult learners she delights in sharing the writing process with others.